# Grýla's Naughty List

*A Yuletide Tale of
Second Chances*

First Edition
Grýla's Naughty List
A Tale of Yule & Second Chances

Copyright © 2024 by Uniquely Iceland
DBA of Consultingly, LLC

Author, Cover, Designer, Typography
Adam J. Lambert-Gorwyn

Imprint
Independently Published

ISBN: 979-8-34059-651-2

## Author's Note

# "Wisdom is welcome wherever it comes from."

Snorri Sturluson
(13th-century historian and poet)
— From The Prose Edda

 **the Yule Lads**

Pictures of the Yule Lads are hidden in this book. Can you find them all?

- Stekkjastaur – Sheep-Cote Clod
- Giljagaur – Gully Gawk
- Stúfur – Stubby
- Þvörusleikir – Spoon-Licker
- Pottasleikir – Pot-Licker
- Askasleikir – Bowl-Licker
- Hurðaskellir – Door-Slammer
- Skyrgámur – Skyr-Gobbler
- Bjúgnakrækir – Sausage-Swiper
- Gluggagægir – Window-Peeper
- Gáttaþefur – Doorway-Sniffer
- Ketkrókur – Meat-Hook
- Kertasníkir – Candle-Stealer

# Chapter 1: The Legend of Grýla & the Yule Lads

*Thump, thump, THUMP!*

The ground shook under the weight of something enormous, something ancient. The wind howled through the mountains of Iceland, as if even nature itself whispered warnings about the one who dwelled in the highlands—Grýla, the ogress of Yule.

"Listen closely, little ones," said the old fisherman, his voice low and gravelly. He sat by the fire, his eyes twinkling with a mixture of mischief and seriousness. The children gathered around, their eyes wide with a blend of excitement and fear. "For many years, children have feared the coming of Grýla. She is no ordinary creature, no simple troll. Oh no... she has the power to find the naughty among us, the ones who refuse to listen to their parents, who are greedy, selfish, or unkind."

*Crunch! Crunch! Crunch!*

"She walks with feet as big as tree stumps, and every step of hers can be heard from miles away. With her comes a sack, a big one, large enough to carry every naughty child in the land. She finds them, and when she does..." the fisherman paused dramatically, leaning in closer, "she scoops them up, and off they go to her cave in the mountains, where they are never seen again!"

*Gasp!*

But it wasn't just Grýla who sent shivers down the spines

of children during Yule. She had help, of course—her mischievous sons, the Yule Lads. Thirteen of them, to be exact, each more troublesome than the last. They didn't kidnap children like their mother, but they caused plenty of chaos.

"First, there's Stekkjastaur, the sheep-cote clod!" the fisherman began, his voice animated. "He loves to sneak into barns and harass the poor sheep. He's got two stiff legs, so clomp, clomp (parents, knock on the floor) you can always hear him coming. Then there's Giljagaur—he hides in the cowshed and drinks all the milk! And Stúfur, the smallest of the lads, sneaks around stealing pans to lick whatever's left. But don't let his size fool you—he's as sneaky as they come!"

The children's eyes grew wider, imagining each Yule Lad, creeping about Iceland in the dark, cold nights leading up to Christmas. The fire crackled, casting shadows that danced across the room like the playful Yule Lads themselves.

"For years, these lads have been up to their tricks, and every Yule, children hope they don't end up on Grýla's Naughty List," the fisherman continued, his voice softer now, almost like a warning. "That's the list you don't want to be on. If you're kind and helpful, you'll have nothing to worry about. But if you misbehave…"

Whoooooosh!

The door of the small cabin rattled, and the wind outside howled as if echoing the fisherman's last words. "If you misbehave," he said again, his voice now just a whisper,

"Grýla will know. She always knows."

But the Yule Lads weren't always so wicked. The fisherman leaned back, his expression thoughtful. "Not many know this, but once upon a time, the Yule Lads weren't just troublemakers. Long ago, before Grýla's heart hardened completely, there was still some kindness left in them. And this Yule… well, something is changing."

The children exchanged puzzled glances. Changing? The Yule Lads were set in their ways, weren't they? Mischief and mayhem were part of their nature. But the old fisherman knew something more—something he wasn't quite ready to share just yet.

"Yule is a time of wonder," he continued, his tone lighter now, "and just as we prepare for Christmas, so do the Yule Lads. But this year, there are whispers—whispers that Grýla's Naughty List isn't as long as it used to be."

Tap, tap, tap!

"You see, some children who were destined to be on that list… well, they seem to be changing. And do you know why?"

The children shook their heads, eager to know the secret.

"It seems," the fisherman said, his eyes gleaming with a hint of hope, "that the Yule Lads are up to something different this year. Perhaps they're tired of the same old tricks. Perhaps…" and here he paused again for dramatic effect, "they've learned that mischief isn't the only thing that brings them joy."

"Now, I've heard that Stekkjastaur, the very first of them, has started his own mission," the fisherman said, his voice full of excitement. "A mission not to cause trouble, but to give children a second chance. I won't spoil the story, but keep an ear out. You might hear clomp, clomp in the night, and it might not be mischief he's bringing this year."

The fire began to dwindle, the logs cracking softly as the fisherman finished his tale for the night. He gazed at the children, their faces lit with curiosity and just a touch of wonder.

"Remember this, little ones," he said kindly. "Yule is not just about gifts and feasts. It's about kindness, about the chance to change, even for the naughtiest of us. And who knows… perhaps even Grýla herself will learn that sometimes, second chances are the greatest gift of all."

The children, once fearful of Grýla and her sons, now felt a strange sense of hope. If the Yule Lads were changing, maybe, just maybe, even Grýla wasn't beyond redemption. Yule was a time of magic, after all.

And with that final thought, the fisherman's voice faded into the soft crackling of the fire. The wind outside had calmed, and the once eerie night now felt warm and safe. Tomorrow was another day of Yule adventures, but tonight, they would dream not of fear, but of the possibilities that lay within a second chance.

## Chapter 2: Stekkjastaur's Lesson in Compassion

*Clomp, clomp, clomp!*

The heavy thud of two stiff legs echoed across the quiet valley. Stekkjastaur, the first of the Yule Lads, was on a mission. His usual routine of sneaking into barns to trouble the sheep had been interrupted this Yule season. There was something different in the air, something he couldn't quite put his finger on.

The icy wind whipped through the hills as Stekkjastaur paused, his tall figure silhouetted against the snowy landscape. The sheep were gathered in a small pen below, their wool thick and warm. Normally, Stekkjastaur would already be clambering over the fence, causing chaos and delighting in the animals' panicked bleats. But this time, he stayed still, his stiff legs barely able to move in the cold.

*Whoooooosh!*

The wind howled around him, but Stekkjastaur wasn't listening. His eyes were fixed on a small figure trudging through the snow, just beyond the pen. A boy, no older than eight or nine winters, was walking alongside the fence, his head down and his arms folded tightly against the biting cold. His name was Bjarni.

*Crunch, crunch, crunch.*

The boy's boots sank deep into the snow, and his breath puffed out in small clouds, almost like the smoke from the chimney of a distant cottage. Stekkjastaur watched as Bjarni stopped by the pen, his face drawn in a scowl as he looked at the sheep.

"You useless creatures," Bjarni muttered, kicking the fence lightly. "I hate you all."

Stekkjastaur raised an eyebrow. Now, this was interesting.

*Thump!*

Stekkjastaur's stiff legs made a heavy sound as he stepped closer, though Bjarni was too lost in his own world to notice. The Yule Lad's ears perked up as the boy continued to grumble under his breath.

"Always getting me in trouble," Bjarni complained, glaring at the sheep. "Father makes me watch you all day. Stupid animals." He gave the fence another light kick, though it was more out of frustration than actual anger.

Stekkjastaur leaned on the fence, his long arms hanging over the wooden posts as he watched the boy closely. This wasn't the kind of mischief he liked to see. It wasn't fun, not like sneaking into barns and scaring sheep. This was... sadness. Bjarni wasn't naughty; he was just hurt.

*Clomp, clomp, clomp!*

Stekkjastaur moved a little closer, finally catching the boy's attention.

Bjarni gasped, stumbling back as his eyes widened in shock. "Wh-who are you?" he stammered, his breath catching in his throat.

Stekkjastaur tilted his head. "You don't know me, boy?" he said, his voice deep and rumbling. "I'm Stekkjastaur, the first of the Yule Lads. And what's this I hear about you hating these sheep?"

Bjarni blinked, confused. "You're... one of the Yule Lads?" he asked, his voice trembling slightly. "But you're not supposed to be real."

Stekkjastaur grinned, showing a row of crooked teeth. "Real enough to hear what you've been saying," he replied. "Real enough to know you're in trouble."

The boy's face paled. "Trouble? But I—"

"Shush," Stekkjastaur interrupted, holding up a hand. "It's not what you think. You're not on Grýla's Naughty List just yet. But," he said, his voice growing serious, "you're on the edge. And do you know why?"

Bjarni shook his head slowly, his eyes still wide.

Stekkjastaur gestured toward the sheep, their soft bleating filling the cold air. "It's not because of what you said," the Yule Lad explained, "but because of what you feel. You've been unkind to them, haven't you? You treat them like they're nothing but a burden."

Bjarni hung his head, shame creeping up his face.

"They're just sheep," he muttered. "Why should I care?"

Stekkjastaur leaned in closer, his stiff legs creaking as he crouched beside the boy. "Let me tell you something, Bjarni. These sheep, they rely on you. They can't protect themselves from the cold or the wolves or even getting lost in the snow. Without someone to care for them, they wouldn't make it through the winter. And you're that someone."

The boy looked up, confusion flickering in his eyes. "But Father only makes me do it because I'm the youngest," he protested. "It's not fair."

Hmph! Stekkjastaur snorted. "Life isn't always fair, boy. But kindness doesn't come from what's fair. It comes from what's right. And right now, those sheep need you."

Bjarni frowned, glancing at the sheep again. "But how do I show them kindness?" he asked, his voice small. "They don't even understand me."

Stekkjastaur smiled, though his crooked grin was more comforting than mischievous this time. "They don't need to understand your words, Bjarni. They understand your actions. Feed them well, keep them warm, and they'll know. Trust me, they'll know."

Bjarni hesitated, then stepped toward the pen. The sheep huddled together, their breaths visible in the cold air. Slowly, carefully, the boy reached out and touched one of the sheep's thick woolly backs. It bleated softly, nuzzling its nose into his hand.

Baaaah! the sheep bleated.

Bjarni's face softened, and for the first time, Stekkjastaur saw a flicker of something new in the boy's eyes—compassion.

The Yule Lad stood tall again, his stiff legs creaking as he did. "That's more like it," he said, his voice full of approval. "You're starting to understand, Bjarni. Kindness doesn't always come naturally. Sometimes you have to learn it, just like you're learning now."

Bjarni nodded, his hand still resting on the sheep. "I didn't know it could feel like this," he admitted quietly. "I never thought about them needing me."

Stekkjastaur crossed his arms, looking satisfied. "Now you're thinking like someone who belongs off Grýla's list," he said. "Keep this up, and you won't have to worry about her sack."

The boy shuddered at the thought, but then he smiled—a small, hopeful smile. "Thank you," he said softly, looking up at the Yule Lad. "For helping me see that."

Stekkjastaur gave him a sharp nod. "Don't thank me yet, boy. There's still work to be done. Keep showing that kindness, not just to the sheep, but to everyone. Your father, your neighbors. You'll see how it changes things."

The Yule Lad turned to leave, but paused just before stepping away. He glanced over his shoulder, a twinkle of mischief still alive in his eyes. "Oh, and Bjarni," he said with a grin, "next time I visit, don't be surprised if I help myself to a little fun with the sheep again. Old habits die hard, you know."

*Clomp, clomp, clomp!*

His stiff-legged steps echoed once more as he disappeared into the snowy night, leaving Bjarni standing by the fence, a new warmth in his heart.

The boy looked back at the sheep, who were now calm and quiet, huddling together for warmth. He smiled and whispered, "I'll take care of you. I promise."

And for the first time in a long while, Bjarni felt proud of his place in the world, understanding that even the smallest acts of kindness could make a great difference.

# Chapter 3: Giljagaur's Milk of Generosity

*Drip, drip, drip!*

The soft sound of water melting from the icicles hanging on the eaves of a small farmhouse filled the crisp winter air. Inside, the warmth of the hearth wrapped the room in a comforting glow, but not everyone felt the warmth in their hearts.

At the long wooden table sat Inga, her arms crossed, a frown creasing her forehead. Her two younger siblings, Svein and Marta, sat across from her, looking longingly at the small bowl of milk that stood in front of Inga. Their eyes, wide and pleading, followed every motion of her hand as she hovered over the bowl.

"I found it first," Inga said defiantly. "So, it's mine."

The siblings exchanged sad glances. It had been a harsh winter, and milk was a luxury these days. Their parents had gone out into the village to trade for supplies, leaving the children to fend for themselves until they returned. The pantry was nearly bare, and the milk in front of Inga was the last they had.

*Clink!*

The spoon hit the side of the bowl as Inga took a sip, savoring the rich taste of the milk. She didn't even look at her brother and sister as they sat in silence, their empty stomachs rumbling.

*Tap, tap, tap!*

The sound of soft footsteps came from outside, but Inga didn't notice. Her mind was too focused on the precious milk in front of her.

Out in the cold, Giljagaur, the second of the Yule Lads, crouched by the window. His usual trick was sneaking into cow sheds and drinking the milk himself, but today, something else caught his attention. Through the frosted glass, he could see Inga sitting at the table, her face set in stubbornness while her siblings sat hungry.

*Hmph!*

Giljagaur snorted quietly to himself. "Selfish, that one," he muttered. He had seen this kind of thing before. Inga wasn't a bad child, not exactly. But her heart had become hard, like the frozen ground outside, and she had forgotten the joy of sharing.

It was time to change that.

With a quick movement, Giljagaur slipped through the door, which creaked ever so slightly.

*Creeeak!*

None of the children heard him. He was, after all, a master of sneaking into places unnoticed.

He tiptoed closer to the table, his sharp eyes fixed on

12

Inga. The bowl of milk was almost empty now, and her brother and sister were watching with sad eyes. Giljagaur frowned.

*Slurp!*

He made a loud sucking noise, startling Inga. She whipped her head around, her eyes wide. "What was that?"

*Thump!*

Giljagaur's stiff boots hit the floor as he stepped out from behind the cupboard. Inga gasped, her eyes growing even wider as the tall figure of the Yule Lad came into view. His wild hair stuck out from under his cap, and his long arms reached down toward the bowl of milk.

"What... what are you doing here?" Inga stammered, shrinking back in her chair.

Giljagaur crossed his arms, his eyebrows raised. "I could ask you the same thing," he said in a deep, gravelly voice. "But it seems I already know. You've got all the milk to yourself while your siblings sit there with empty bowls."

Inga flushed red, her eyes darting to the nearly empty bowl. "It's mine," she muttered defensively. "I found it."

*Clunk!*

Giljagaur's heavy boots stomped on the wooden floor as he moved closer, shaking his head slowly. "Found it, did you? Well, that may be true, but Yule is no time to hoard what little you have. Yule is a time for sharing, Inga."

The girl blinked up at him, confusion flickering across her face. "But there's barely enough for me," she said. "How can I share when there's not enough?"

Giljagaur crouched down beside her, his voice softening. "Ah, but that's where you're wrong, little one. Sharing isn't about having plenty. It's about giving what you can, even when there's little to give."

Inga's frown deepened. She had heard adults talk about sharing before, but it had always seemed like something they expected her to do without understanding why. "But... if I share, I won't have any left."

Huff! Giljagaur let out a small puff of air. "You think so? Well, let me show you something." He reached out his long fingers and gently lifted the bowl of milk from the table. With a quick flick of his wrist, he poured a tiny amount of milk into each of the other two empty bowls in front of Svein and Marta.

Inga gasped. "That wasn't enough for them!" she exclaimed. "They'll still be hungry."

But as she spoke, something strange happened. The bowls, though only holding a few drops of milk, didn't look quite as empty as they should have. In fact, they seemed fuller than they had been before. And as her siblings took their spoons and dipped them into the
14

bowls, the milk didn't disappear as quickly as it should have.

Slurp, slurp! Svein and Marta sipped the milk, their eyes lighting up with surprise. "It's so good!" Marta exclaimed, her face breaking into a smile. Svein nodded in agreement, a happy grin spreading across his face.

Inga stared, her mouth slightly open. "But... how is that possible?"

Giljagaur smiled slyly, his sharp eyes twinkling. "That's the magic of sharing, Inga," he said. "When you give what little you have, you find that it somehow becomes more than enough."

Inga blinked, still trying to process what she had just seen. "But... what about my bowl?" she asked, looking down at the nearly empty dish in front of her.

Giljagaur stood up, his long legs creaking as he rose. "Take a look for yourself," he said, stepping back from the table.

Hesitantly, Inga glanced down at her bowl. To her astonishment, it wasn't empty anymore. The milk had returned—fuller, creamier, and more abundant than it had been before she shared it with her siblings.

Inga's eyes filled with wonder. "How... how did it do that?" she whispered.

Giljagaur grinned, his crooked teeth showing as he

crossed his arms again. "It's the magic of generosity, Inga. When you share, the joy you give others comes back to you. Sometimes it's in ways you don't expect. That's the secret of Yule. It's not about what you keep for yourself—it's about what you give to others."

Inga looked up at him, her heart softening as the warmth of his words sank in. She smiled, a real smile this time, and without another word, she picked up her spoon and shared the last of her milk with Svein and Marta.

*Clink, clink, clink!*

Their spoons hit the bowls as they sipped happily, the once tense room now filled with the sound of satisfied slurps and quiet giggles.

Giljagaur nodded, pleased with the change he had sparked in Inga's heart. "Well," he said, stretching his long arms above his head, "I think my work here is done."

The Yule Lad turned to leave, his footsteps soft as he moved toward the door. But before he stepped out into the snow, he looked back over his shoulder, a playful glint in his eye.

"Remember, Inga," he said, "next time you have something worth sharing, don't hesitate. The more you give, the more you'll find waiting for you in return."

*Creak!*

The door closed behind him, leaving the three children in the warm glow of the hearth.

Inga watched the door for a moment, her heart full of something she hadn't felt in a long time—joy. She had learned something important today, something she knew she wouldn't forget. Sharing, even when you have little, could make your heart feel fuller than any bowl of milk ever could.

## Chapter 4: Grýla's Suspicion

*Whooooooosh!*

The wind howled outside Grýla's dark and foreboding cave, the icy cold biting at the rocks like hungry wolves. Deep inside, Grýla stirred, her sharp eyes scanning the walls of her cavernous home. She sat by a cauldron, stirring its thick, bubbling contents with a massive spoon, but her mind was elsewhere.

Something wasn't right.

*Thud! Thud! Thud!*

Her heavy footsteps echoed through the cave as she paced back and forth. Every year, her Naughty List was long—filled with names of children who had misbehaved, acted selfishly, or been unkind. And every year, she prepared her sack, ready to collect those who had crossed the line and bring them back to her cave. But this year…

*Rustle!*

She grabbed the long scroll of parchment that was her Naughty List and unrolled it in front of her. Her frown deepened as her eyes scanned the names. There were still children on the list, of course. There were always some. But the list wasn't nearly as long as it should be.

*Thump!*

She slammed the scroll down on the table, her massive hands gripping the edges. "What is going on?" she growled, her voice rumbling like thunder. "Where are all the naughty children?"

Grýla's sharp ears twitched as she heard the distant laughter of children outside her cave, down in the valley. They were supposed to be afraid of her, hiding indoors, making last-minute attempts to be good in hopes of staying off her list. But this year, something was different. There was less fear, less mischief, and it made her uneasy.

Her long, bony fingers drummed on the table as she thought. Could it be that fewer children were misbehaving this Yule? That couldn't be right. Grýla had lived for hundreds of years, and children had always been the same—prone to naughtiness, selfishness, and carelessness.

*Hiiisssss!*

The fire under her cauldron flared up, casting strange shadows on the walls of the cave. Grýla scowled as the flames danced in the reflection of her black, beady eyes. She couldn't shake the feeling that something, or someone, was behind this change.

The Yule Lads.

Her sons.

Grýla stopped pacing and stood still, her mind working quickly. The Yule Lads were known for their tricks and mischief, but lately, she had noticed something strange about them too. They had been quieter, less troublesome, sneaking off to who-knows-where. Grýla had assumed they were just up to their usual antics, but now... now she wasn't so sure.

*Crunch! Crunch! Crunch!*

She stomped her way to the mouth of the cave, the snow beneath her feet crackling like dry bones. From her vantage point high in the mountains, she could see the village below. The lights from the small houses twinkled like stars, and the faint sound of children's laughter carried on the wind.

Grýla narrowed her eyes. What were her sons up to? Had they forgotten their purpose? Had they become soft?

*Grrrrr!*

A low growl escaped her throat as she turned and stomped back inside, her mind racing. She had taught her sons to be tricksters, to keep children on their toes, to cause trouble. That was their nature! And yet, the Naughty List was shrinking. It made no sense.

Grýla strode to the back of the cave, where her sons' quarters were. The walls were covered in rough carvings and old Yule decorations, the remnants of many past winters. She reached the large wooden door and BAM! threw it open, her eyes darting from one side of the room to the other.

Empty. The room was empty. No Stekkjastaur. No Giljagaur. No Stúfur. Not a single one of her sons was there.

*Whaaam!*

She slammed the door shut behind her, her teeth grinding in frustration. "Where are those boys?" she muttered under her breath.

Grýla stomped back to her cauldron and sat down heavily on her stone stool. The steam rising from the pot filled the air with the smell of herbs and spices, but she barely noticed. Her mind was focused on one thing now—figuring out why her Naughty List was shorter than ever and what her Yule Lads were doing to cause it.

She sat still for a moment, her eyes narrowing as an idea took shape in her mind. Her instincts told her something was wrong, and her instincts were never wrong. The Yule Lads had to be behind this, and Grýla was determined to find out how.

*Tap, tap, tap.*

Her long nails drummed on the edge of the cauldron as she began to plot her next move. "If they think they can fool me, they've got another thing coming," she said to herself, her voice cold and sharp.

Grýla wasn't one to let things slide. She had a reputation to maintain, after all, and she wasn't about to let her Naughty List disappear without a fight. Whatever her sons were up to, she would uncover their secrets. And when she did, there would be consequences.

The fire beneath the cauldron roared, casting flickering light across Grýla's grim face as she leaned forward, deep in thought. "Those boys better have a good reason for this," she muttered. "Or they'll be the next ones on my Naughty List."

# Chapter 5: The Yule Lads' New Mission

*Clomp, clomp, clomp!*

Stekkjastaur's stiff-legged steps echoed through the narrow pass as he made his way back to the secret meeting spot. The moon shone bright in the sky, casting long shadows on the snowy ground. He had just returned from helping Bjarni with his sheep and felt a strange warmth in his chest that he hadn't felt in years.

Ahead, in the clearing beneath an ancient pine tree, the other Yule Lads were already gathered, their figures dark and huddled under the bare branches. Stekkjastaur grinned. The plan was coming together.

*Crunch, crunch, crunch!*

His boots sank into the snow as he joined the group, and the lads looked up, nodding in acknowledgment. Giljagaur, the second eldest, was leaning against a tree, his mischievous eyes twinkling. Stúfur, the smallest of the brothers, was pacing back and forth, his tiny feet barely making a sound.

"Well?" Giljagaur asked, his voice low but eager. "How did it go?"

Stekkjastaur's grin widened. "Better than expected. The boy, Bjarni—he's not on the Naughty List anymore. Showed him some compassion for the sheep, and I think he learned something."

Giljagaur chuckled. "Compassion? Coming from you? Now that's something I'd never thought I'd see."

Stekkjastaur shrugged, still smiling. "We all change, brother. And speaking of change, I've noticed something since we started this new mission." He paused, glancing at each of his brothers. "We're making a difference. The children we've helped—they're not just scared of ending up on Grýla's list. They're learning. They're changing."

The group fell silent for a moment, each Yule Lad reflecting on the work they had begun. It had all started when Stekkjastaur, tired of the same old tricks, suggested something new. What if, instead of scaring and tricking children, they helped them change? What if they gave them second chances, just like the spirit of Yule?

It hadn't been an easy decision. The Yule Lads were tricksters by nature, and mischief was in their blood. But as the years went by, they had seen the same names appear on Grýla's Naughty List over and over again. The same children making the same mistakes.

"Stekkjastaur's right," Giljagaur said, pushing away from the tree. "I helped Inga and her siblings today. She was hoarding the last of their milk, but after a little nudge in the right direction, she shared it. And you know what?" He smiled, a rare, genuine smile. "It made her happier."

Stúfur nodded, his tiny hands clasped in front of him. "I've been thinking about my mission too," he piped up, his voice small but firm. "There's a boy in town, Kári. Lazy as can be. But I've got a plan. I'm going to show him how even the smallest acts of help can make a big difference."

The Yule Lads all turned to look at him, nodding in approval. The change in their hearts had begun quietly, but now it was starting to take shape, and they were all beginning to feel it.

"We've been up to mischief for centuries," Stekkjastaur said, his voice thoughtful. "And it was fun, don't get me wrong. But this... this feels different. Better."

*Clink, clank, clunk!*

The sound of something hitting the ice behind them made the group turn. From the shadows stepped Þvörusleikir, his long, thin figure barely visible in the darkness. He had a wooden spoon tucked under his arm, his usual prize from sneaking into kitchens. "Did I hear something about changing hearts?" he asked, his voice full of curiosity.

Stekkjastaur grinned. "You heard right, Þvörusleikir. We've got a new mission this year."

The Yule Lad raised an eyebrow, his hand absently stroking the spoon. "And what might that be?"

Stekkjastaur stepped forward, his stiff legs crunching the snow beneath him. "We're giving second chances. Instead of just playing tricks and scaring children, we're helping them. If they're on Grýla's Naughty List, we're showing them a better way. We're giving them a chance to change before she finds them."

Þvörusleikir stared at him, then glanced at the other lads. "And you're all in on this?"

Giljagaur shrugged, a mischievous grin still playing on his lips. "It's not our usual style, but I've gotta admit, it's been rewarding."

Stúfur nodded enthusiastically. "It's true! I've seen it myself. We're making a difference!"

Þvörusleikir rubbed his chin, thinking it over. "And what about Grýla? You know she won't be happy when she finds out we've been interfering with her list."

The group went quiet again. They all knew Grýla's temper. She had been keeping track of naughty children for as long as they could remember, and she was fierce about it. If she found out that her sons were helping children get off her list instead of ensuring they stayed on it, there would be trouble.

"We'll deal with Grýla when the time comes," Stekkjastaur said firmly. "For now, we focus on the children. It's Yule, and Yule is about second chances. Even for us."

The others nodded slowly, though there was still a flicker of unease in the air. They knew they were walking a dangerous line, but there was no turning back now.

*Whoooosh!*

A cold wind whipped through the clearing, and the Yule

Lads shivered. Stekkjastaur pulled his thick coat tighter around him and looked out toward the village below. "We've got work to do," he said quietly. "There's still time before Yule is over, and there are still children who need us."

Giljagaur cracked his knuckles. "Well, I'm not one to sit around. Who's next on your list?"

The group huddled closer as Stekkjastaur pulled out a small, worn piece of parchment from his pocket. It wasn't Grýla's Naughty List—it was their own. A list of children who needed help, not punishment. They had started it in secret, each Yule Lad adding names as they found children in need of a second chance.

Stúfur pointed to one of the names on the list. "Kári," he said. "He's next."

The others nodded, and without another word, they scattered into the night, their footsteps light as they moved through the snow. Their mission was clear, and time was running short. They had to help as many children as they could before Grýla found out what they were doing.

*Crunch, crunch, crunch!*

Their steps grew fainter as they disappeared into the shadows, each heading toward a different house, ready to change another heart.

In the silence that followed, the ancient pine tree stood

alone, its branches swaying gently in the cold night air. The Yule Lads were no longer just mischievous tricksters. They were something more now—bringers of second chances, of hope, of Yule's true spirit.

And though the path ahead was uncertain, they knew one thing for sure: this was a Yule they would never forget.

# Chapter 6: Stúfur's Tiny Gift of Helpfulness

*Pitter, patter, pitter, patter, pitter, patter!*

The soft sound of tiny footsteps barely broke the stillness of the snowy night. Stúfur, the smallest of the Yule Lads, crept silently through the narrow alleyways of the village. His mission was simple, yet crucial—help Kári, a boy who had earned a reputation for his laziness, learn the value of being helpful.

Stúfur's small size made him perfect for slipping unnoticed into homes, but tonight he wasn't sneaking in to steal food or make mischief. No, tonight he had a more important task.

*Pitter, patter, pitter, patter, pitter patter!*

His little feet skittered over the cobblestones as he approached Kári's house. The boy lived with his parents in a small cottage near the edge of the village, and from what Stúfur had heard, Kári never lifted a finger to help around the house. His parents worked hard, especially during the harsh winter months, but Kári preferred to sit by the fire, reading or playing with his wooden toys, while chores piled up.

*Whoosh!*

The wind rustled through the trees as Stúfur stopped by the window, peeking in through the frosted glass. Inside, the dim glow of a lantern illuminated the small, warm room. Kári sat by the hearth, a book in his hands and a blanket draped over his shoulders. The fire crackled softly, casting dancing shadows on the walls. His mother bustled about in the kitchen, chopping vegetables and stirring a pot, while his father sat in a chair, mending a torn fishing net. Both looked tired.

Kári, however, was oblivious to the work around him. He was lost in his book, as he often was.

*Hmph!*

Stúfur crossed his tiny arms, frowning in disapproval. "Lazy boy," he muttered to himself. "If he doesn't change, Grýla's sack will be waiting for him."

With a quick leap, Stúfur scrambled up the wall and slipped through the narrow chimney, landing softly in the hearth. Puff! A cloud of soot rose as he landed, but no one noticed. He was, after all, very small.

Stúfur watched from the shadows for a moment, his tiny eyes narrowing as he studied the scene. Kári's mother wiped her brow, clearly exhausted, while his father sighed heavily as he worked on the net. Yet Kári remained motionless, absorbed in his book.

Stúfur decided it was time for a little nudge.

*Creeeeak!*

The floorboards groaned as Stúfur crept closer to Kári's side, careful not to make a sound. He waited until the boy turned a page in his book, and then, with a quick flick of his tiny hand, Stúfur knocked the blanket from Kári's shoulders.

*Kerpuff!*

The blanket fell to the floor.

Kári blinked in surprise and glanced down at the fallen blanket. For a moment, he seemed confused, but then he shrugged and reached down to pick it up.

But before he could grab it, Stúfur nudged it just out of reach.

*Whoooosh!*

The blanket slid across the floor, and Kári's brow furrowed in frustration. "That's odd," he muttered. He got up from his chair and bent down to retrieve the blanket again, but once more, Stúfur nudged it out of his grasp, sending it sliding toward the door.

"Hey!" Kári exclaimed, standing up and following the blanket across the room. He was halfway to the door when he paused, noticing his mother struggling with the heavy pot on the stove.

Kári sighed. "Do you need help with that, Mother?" he asked, his voice reluctant.

His mother glanced up in surprise. "Oh, Kári, that would be wonderful. It's quite heavy."

Stúfur watched from the shadows, his tiny heart racing with excitement. Kári had taken the first step—he had offered to help. Now it was time to see if he would follow through.

*Klink, clank, clunk!*

The pot rattled as Kári lifted it carefully, bringing it over to the table where his mother had set out bowls for dinner. His mother smiled at him warmly, her tired eyes brightening. "Thank you, my boy. That was very kind of you."

Kári nodded, though he still seemed more interested in returning to his book than in helping. But Stúfur wasn't done yet.

The tiny Yule Lad skittered across the floor, making his way toward the broom that stood in the corner. With a quick flick of his hand, he knocked the broom over, sending it clattering to the floor.

*Thump!*

Kári turned around, startled. "What's going on tonight?" he muttered. He walked over to the broom, bending down to pick it up. As he did, his father looked up from his mending.

"Would you mind sweeping the floor, Kári?" his father asked, his voice hopeful. "It's getting awfully dirty in here with all the snow we've tracked in."

Kári hesitated, his hand hovering over the broom. His gaze flicked toward the book he had left by the fire, but something in his father's weary expression made him pause.

"All right," Kári said with a sigh. He took the broom in his hands and began to sweep the floor, slowly at first, but then with more care as he noticed how much dirt and soot had collected near the hearth.

*Swish, swish, swish!*

The sound of the broom bristles sweeping across the floor filled the room, and Kári found himself lost in the rhythm of the task. As he swept, he began to notice things he hadn't before—the little scuff marks near the door, the crumbs that had fallen from the table, the soot scattered around the hearth.

His parents continued with their own work, and for the first time in a long while, Kári felt a sense of quiet satisfaction. The floor, which had seemed so messy before, was starting to look clean again.

Stúfur watched from the shadows, his tiny heart swelling with pride. This was it. This was the moment Kári had needed—a chance to see that even small acts of helpfulness made a big difference.

Kári finished sweeping and leaned the broom against the wall. He glanced around the room, taking in the quiet, warm atmosphere. His mother had finished cooking, and his father had just finished mending the net. Dinner was ready, and for the first time, Kári felt like he had contributed to the warmth and comfort of the home.

He sat down at the table, a small smile playing on his lips. His mother placed a bowl of stew in front of him, and his father clapped him on the shoulder.

"Thank you for your help, Kári," his father said kindly. "It's good to have you pitch in."

Kári nodded, feeling a strange warmth in his chest. "It wasn't so bad," he admitted quietly.

Stúfur, still hidden in the shadows, smiled to himself. His mission was complete. Kári wasn't lazy at heart—he just needed to see how good it felt to be helpful.

Tap, tap, tap!

Stúfur's tiny feet skittered back toward the hearth as he prepared to leave. Before slipping up the chimney, he took one last glance at Kári, who was now happily chatting with his parents as they ate dinner together.

"One more name off the Naughty List," Stúfur whispered to himself, his tiny voice full of satisfaction. "That's the power of being helpful."

Whooosh!

With a soft puff of soot, Stúfur disappeared up the chimney, leaving the cozy home behind him.

Outside, the cold night air wrapped around him as he made his way through the snow, heading back to the secret meeting spot where his brothers were waiting. The Yule Lads' mission was working. One child at a time, they were giving second chances—and it felt better than any mischief they had ever caused.

# Chapter 7: Þvörusleikir's Spoon of Honesty

*Thwack! Thwack! Thwack!*

The wooden spoon hit the sides of the pot rhythmically as Anna stirred the thick porridge on the stove. Her mother had asked her to keep an eye on dinner while she ran to the market, but Anna's mind was elsewhere. Her eyes kept drifting toward the small basket on the counter, filled with freshly baked pastries.

*Sniff, sniff, sniff.*

The sweet smell of cinnamon and sugar filled the kitchen, making Anna's stomach rumble. The pastries were for dessert, and her mother had made it clear that they were not to be touched until after dinner. But Anna, who was known for her mischievous ways, wasn't one to always follow the rules.

She had a habit of telling little lies—small, seemingly harmless things. If she broke something, she'd say her brother did it. If she ate the last piece of bread, she'd claim the dog snatched it. It wasn't that she wanted to be dishonest, exactly. It just seemed easier to avoid trouble by bending the truth.

*Thwack, thwack, thwack!*

The spoon hit the pot again, but this time Anna stopped stirring. Her eyes locked on the pastries, and her fingers itched to grab one.

"No one will notice if I take just one," she whispered to herself. "Mother won't be back for a while."

*Whoooosh!*

A gust of wind rustled the curtains, but Anna didn't notice. Her focus was entirely on the basket of pastries.

What she didn't see, however, was the tall, thin figure slipping through the crack in the door. Þvörusleikir, the Yule Lad known for licking spoons, was watching her. His long, bony fingers clutched a wooden spoon, and his sharp eyes gleamed with curiosity. He had heard of Anna's little fibs, and tonight, he was here to teach her a valuable lesson.

*Creak, thud.*

The door closed softly behind him as Þvörusleikir moved closer to the counter. Anna, still unaware of his presence, reached for the basket, her hand hovering just above the golden-brown pastries.

But before she could take one, slap! Þvörusleikir's spoon tapped her hand lightly. Anna yelped in surprise, pulling her hand back as she looked around, her heart racing. "Who... who's there?"

"Just me," came a deep, raspy voice.

Anna spun around, her eyes widening as she saw the tall, thin figure standing by the hearth. His long arms reached almost to the floor, and in one hand, he held a long wooden spoon, just like the one she'd been using to stir the porridge.

"W-who are you?" she stammered, taking a step back.

Þvörusleikir grinned, showing a row of crooked teeth. "I'm Þvörusleikir," he said, his voice full of mischief. "And I know exactly what you were about to do."

Anna's face flushed red, and she quickly tried to deny it. "I wasn't going to do anything! I was just... checking the pastries to make sure they're ready for after dinner."

Þvörusleikir raised an eyebrow, tapping his spoon thoughtfully against the side of the table. Tap, tap. "Is that so?" he said, his tone playful. "And here I thought you were about to sneak one for yourself before anyone else could have a taste."

Anna's heart pounded in her chest, but she crossed her arms and lifted her chin, trying to look confident. "I wasn't going to eat one," she insisted. "I know better than that."

Þvörusleikir stepped closer, his long shadow falling over the basket of pastries. "Lying won't get you very far, you know," he said softly. "Especially not with me. I can always tell when someone isn't being honest."

Anna bit her lip, glancing nervously at the spoon in Þvörusleikir's hand. He wasn't like the adults in her life— he seemed to know more, to see more. She could feel his sharp eyes on her, watching her every move.

For a moment, she considered sticking to her story. She could lie her way out of this, just like she had done so many times before. But something about the way Þvörusleikir looked at her made her hesitate.

"I wasn't going to eat the pastry," she repeated, though her voice wavered.

*Thump!*

Þvörusleikir slammed his spoon onto the table, making Anna jump. "Lying again?" he asked, his voice rising. "That's twice now! How many more times will you try to deceive me?"

Anna's eyes widened in shock. She hadn't expected the Yule Lad to get so angry, but the truth was, she had lied. Twice. And now she was stuck in her own web of dishonesty.

Seeing the panic on her face, Þvörusleikir's expression softened. He crouched down so that his long, thin face was level with hers. "Listen to me, Anna," he said gently. "It's not too late to tell the truth. But the longer you lie, the harder it will be to stop."

Anna blinked, feeling tears prickling at the corners of her eyes. She had always thought that her little lies didn't matter, that they were harmless. But now, standing in front of the strange Yule Lad with the spoon, she realized how wrong she had been.

"I... I was going to eat one," she admitted quietly,

lowering her head. "I didn't think anyone would notice."

Þvörusleikir nodded slowly, a small smile creeping onto his face. "There now," he said softly. "That wasn't so hard, was it?"

Anna shook her head, her cheeks flushed with embarrassment. "I'm sorry," she whispered. "I didn't mean to lie. I just didn't want to get in trouble."

Þvörusleikir stood up, his long arms folding in front of him. "We all make mistakes," he said kindly. "But it's important to remember that honesty is the best way to make things right. When you lie, you create more problems for yourself. But when you tell the truth, even when it's hard, you free yourself from those problems."

Anna sniffled, wiping her eyes with the sleeve of her sweater. "I guess I didn't think about it that way."

The Yule Lad tapped his spoon on the edge of the table again, but this time, the sound was soft and reassuring. Tap, tap."From now on, be honest," he said. "No more fibs, no more little lies. Tell the truth, even when it's difficult. It will make your life a lot easier—and it will keep you off Grýla's Naughty List."

Anna nodded, feeling a strange sense of relief wash over her. It wasn't easy admitting the truth, but now that she had, she felt lighter. The fear of getting caught in another lie had melted away.

"Thank you," she said softly, looking up at Þvörusleikir.

"I'll try to be better."

The Yule Lad grinned, his crooked teeth showing again. "Good. Now, get back to stirring that porridge before it burns!" he said, pointing to the pot on the stove.

Anna smiled and hurried over to the pot, picking up the spoon and giving the porridge a good stir.

*Thwack, thwack, thwaaack!*

She kept her eyes on the food, but a small part of her wondered if she'd imagined the whole thing.

When she glanced back at the basket of pastries, Þvörusleikir was gone. The door to the cottage was slightly ajar, and the cold night air drifted in, carrying with it the sound of the wind.

*Whoooooosh!*

Anna smiled to herself as she stirred the pot. Tonight, she had learned an important lesson. Honesty wasn't always easy, but it was always right. And as she stirred, she made a silent promise to herself—no more lies.

From now on, she would tell the truth, no matter how tempting it was to fib.

# Chapter 8: Grýla's Encounter with the Hidden Folk

*Crunch, crunch, crunch!*

Grýla's heavy boots sank into the snow as she stomped through the icy mountainside. Her black cloak billowed in the wind, and her sharp eyes glinted under her thick fur hood. She was on a mission, and nothing would stop her from getting to the bottom of this strange shrinking Naughty List.

For centuries, children had feared her. Every Yule season, her list grew longer with names of those who misbehaved. But this year, something was different. The names were disappearing, and she had her suspicions about who was behind it. Her sons, the Yule Lads, had been acting strange lately—sneaking off on mysterious errands, helping children instead of scaring them. She had raised them to be tricksters, but now they were meddling with her work.

*Whoooooosh!*

The cold wind whipped through the snow-covered trees, carrying with it a faint whisper—a warning, perhaps, but Grýla didn't care. She was headed to the one place she knew she would find answers: the hidden valley where the Hidden Folk lived.

Grýla had avoided the Hidden Folk for years. They were strange beings—part of the earth and the rocks, old as the mountains themselves. But they were wise, and if anyone knew what was happening with her Yule Lads, it was them.

42

As she approached the valley, the snow seemed to quiet, muffling her footsteps. The entrance to the Hidden Folk's realm was unmarked, but Grýla knew it by the way the air felt thicker, as though the very earth were watching her approach.

*Thump, thump, thump!*

She pounded her fist on a jagged rock, and the sound echoed through the valley.

"I know you're here!" she called out, her voice booming in the stillness. "Come out. I demand answers!"

For a long moment, there was only silence. Grýla stood still, her breath puffing out in small clouds of steam. Then, the rock before her began to shimmer, and from its surface, a doorway appeared, glowing faintly in the cold winter light.

*Whooosh!*

The door opened without a sound, and from within, three figures stepped out. They were tall and slender, their features sharp yet soft, like the edges of a snowflake. Their skin seemed to glow faintly, as if they were made of the very light of the moon.

Grýla crossed her arms, narrowing her eyes at them. "I don't have time for pleasantries," she growled. "Tell me what you know about my sons and the children they've been helping. Why is my Naughty List shrinking?"

The tallest of the Hidden Folk, a woman with long silver hair, stepped forward, her face calm and untroubled by Grýla's anger. "Grýla," she said in a voice that seemed to hum like the wind through the trees, "you come seeking answers, but you may not like what you hear."

Grýla's eyes flashed. "I'm not here for riddles," she snapped. "I want the truth."

The woman nodded, her expression serene. "Very well. The truth is that your sons have chosen a different path this Yule season. They have seen that their tricks no longer bring them joy, and they are helping the children instead."

Grýla clenched her fists, her jaw tightening. "Helping? Why would they do that? They're meant to be tricksters. They're supposed to scare children into behaving!"

The second figure, a man with a cloak woven from the colors of the night sky, spoke up, his voice soft but firm. "Times change, Grýla. Even your sons are not immune to the spirit of Yule. They have seen that fear is not the only way to guide children. Sometimes, kindness can be a more powerful teacher."

*Hmph!*

Grýla scowled. "Kindness? My sons are not kind. They are mischievous, just like me. This is all nonsense."

The third figure, a young man with eyes the color of deep, frozen lakes, stepped forward. He regarded Grýla with a look of sympathy, though his voice was steady. "You may not understand it now, but your sons are giving the children something more important than fear. They are giving them second chances. Yule is a time of renewal, of hope. Even you, Grýla, must see that the world is changing."

Grýla's anger flared, and she took a step forward, her massive frame looming over the Hidden Folk. "The world may change," she growled, "but I do not. I have my role, and the children must fear me if they are to behave. This nonsense of second chances will undo all the work I've done for centuries!"

The woman with the silver hair remained calm, though her gaze held a depth that made Grýla uneasy. "Grýla," she said softly, "have you ever wondered why you cling so tightly to fear? Why you need the children to be afraid of you?"

Grýla blinked, her anger faltering for a moment. "What do you mean?"

The woman took a step closer, her voice low and gentle. "You were not always like this. Once, long ago, you understood kindness. You knew that fear was not the only way to lead. But over the years, your heart hardened. You grew colder, just like the mountains you live in."

Grýla's fists tightened again. "I am not soft. Fear is what keeps the children in line. That is my purpose."

The young man with the lake-blue eyes stepped forward, his voice soft but piercing. "Is it fear that truly guides

them, Grýla, or is it the chance to learn and grow from their mistakes? Your sons have chosen to teach the children the value of second chances, not through punishment, but through lessons of kindness, honesty, and helpfulness."

Grýla's heart pounded in her chest, but she refused to let their words sink in. "I don't need your advice," she snarled. "My sons are interfering with my work. I will set them straight, and the Naughty List will still grow."

The Hidden Folk exchanged glances, but none of them seemed afraid of her. The man with the cloak of stars stepped closer, his voice full of quiet wisdom. "You may do as you wish, Grýla. But know this—there is a warmth spreading through the land this Yule, and it is stronger than any fear you can conjure. The children are learning to change, and even if you refuse to see it, your sons are part of that change."

Grýla's eyes narrowed. "We'll see about that," she muttered darkly. Without another word, she turned on her heel and stormed back the way she had come, the snow crunching beneath her feet.

*Crunch, crunch, crunch!*

The Hidden Folk watched her go, their expressions calm but sad. As Grýla disappeared into the swirling snow, the woman with silver hair sighed softly. "She will have to learn the hard way," she said quietly.

The man with the lake-blue eyes nodded. "But even Grýla is not beyond a second chance."

# Chapter 9: Askasleikir and the Power of Sharing

*Clatter, clatter, clatter!*

The sound of wooden bowls tumbling to the floor echoed through the small house as Lóa hurried around, gathering her toys and treasures. Her younger brother and sister sat nearby, their eyes following her movements with a mixture of hope and frustration.

"Lóa, can we play too?" asked her brother, Páll, his voice soft.

"No!" Lóa snapped, hugging her collection of dolls and shiny stones to her chest. "These are mine! You'll just break them."

Her sister, Sigrún, frowned, her small hands twisting in her lap. "But you never share," she said quietly. "It's not fair."

Lóa scowled. "Life isn't fair, Sigrún. If you wanted toys, you should have asked for them yourself."

The younger children looked down at their empty hands, sadness creeping into their eyes. It wasn't the first time Lóa had refused to share. She had always been possessive of her things, guarding them like treasures, and the idea of letting someone else touch them made her feel uneasy.

But someone else had been watching Lóa, someone who understood the power of sharing better than most.

48

*Scratch, scratch, scratch!*

The sound of long nails on wood filled the air as Askasleikir, the Bowl Licker, crept closer to the house. He was one of the more peculiar Yule Lads, known for sneaking into homes to lick the scraps from wooden bowls left behind after a meal. But tonight, he wasn't looking for scraps of food. He had something far more important in mind.

Askasleikir crouched by the window, his tall, lanky frame almost invisible in the shadows. He peered inside, watching as Lóa clutched her toys while her younger siblings sat with nothing. His sharp eyes narrowed in disapproval.

*Tap, tap, tap!*

He rapped his long fingers against the glass, and Lóa jumped, startled by the sound.

"Who's there?" she asked, her voice shaky. She hurried to the window, but when she peeked outside, she saw nothing but the snow falling gently in the darkness.

"It's just the wind," she muttered, returning to her pile of toys.

But Askasleikir wasn't far. He slipped through the back door, his bare feet barely making a sound as he moved through the shadows. Lóa's back was turned to him, and her siblings were too focused on their own disappointment to notice the strange figure creeping closer.

*Thud!*

Askasleikir dropped a small wooden bowl onto the floor behind Lóa.

She gasped, spinning around, her heart racing. "What... what's that?"

The bowl wobbled on the floor for a moment before settling with a soft clunk. Lóa frowned and walked over to it, picking it up. It was empty, old, and worn, as though it had been used for many years. She turned it over in her hands, confused. "Where did this come from?"

"I brought it," came a voice from the shadows.

Lóa's breath caught in her throat, and she whipped around to see a tall, thin figure emerging from the darkness. His long arms reached the ground, and his sharp features were shadowed in the dim light of the room. She recognized him instantly—Askasleikir, the Bowl Licker.

Lóa backed up, clutching the bowl. "What are you doing here?" she asked, her voice trembling.

Askasleikir grinned, his crooked teeth showing. "I've been watching you, Lóa," he said, his voice low but not unkind. "And I see that you have many things. More than enough."

Lóa's eyes narrowed. "They're mine," she said defiantly. "I don't have to share if I don't want to."

Askasleikir's grin faded, and he crouched down to her level, his long fingers still tapping the edge of the bowl. Tap, tap, tap. "That may be true," he said, "but let me tell you something about this bowl. It's not just any bowl. It's special."

Lóa frowned, confused. "It looks like an old bowl to me."

Askasleikir chuckled softly. "Ah, but that's where you're wrong. This bowl holds a secret—a secret about the power of sharing. You see, Lóa, when you give to others, you don't lose what's yours. Instead, you gain something far more valuable."

Lóa crossed her arms, clearly skeptical. "That doesn't make any sense. If I give something away, I don't have it anymore. How is that gaining anything?"

Askasleikir's eyes twinkled as he set the bowl down on the floor between them. "Let me show you," he said. "Place one of your treasures in the bowl."

Lóa hesitated, her eyes darting between the bowl and the Yule Lad. But curiosity got the better of her, and she reluctantly picked up one of her shiny stones, dropping it into the bowl with a soft plunk.

Askasleikir smiled, his long fingers brushing the edge of the bowl again. Tap, tap. "Now," he said, "give this bowl to your brother."

Lóa blinked in surprise. "What? But that's my stone!"

Askasleikir nodded. "Yes, it is. But remember what I told you. Sharing doesn't mean losing. Trust me."

Lóa frowned but slowly picked up the bowl and walked over to Páll, who was sitting quietly by the fire. "Here," she said, holding out the bowl awkwardly. "You can have this."

Páll's eyes widened in surprise. "Really?"

Lóa nodded, though she still didn't fully understand why she was doing it. "Yes… really."

Páll took the bowl, his small hands trembling slightly as he looked down at the shiny stone inside. His face lit up with a smile, the kind of smile Lóa hadn't seen in a long time. "Thank you!" he said, his voice filled with joy.

Askasleikir's grin widened as he watched the exchange. "Now," he said softly, "look inside your pile."

Lóa glanced back at her pile of toys, her eyes widening in disbelief. There, among her things, was a new shiny stone, even brighter than the one she had given to Páll.

"How… how did that happen?" she whispered, her heart racing.

Askasleikir stood up, his long frame towering over her once more. "That's the magic of sharing, Lóa," he said.

"When you give to others, you find that you are never truly without. The joy you bring to someone else comes back to you, in ways you may not expect."

Lóa stared at the new stone in her hands, her mind whirling. She had never thought of sharing as something that could bring her more joy, but now she saw how happy it had made Páll. And in return, she felt something warm growing in her chest—something she hadn't felt before.

Askasleikir chuckled softly. "It's not just about the things you give, Lóa," he said, his voice gentle. "It's about the joy that sharing brings. The more you share, the more your heart grows."

Lóa looked up at him, her eyes filled with wonder. "I... I think I understand now."

Askasleikir nodded, his sharp features softening. "Good. Now, go on. Share with your sister too."

Without hesitation, Lóa picked up another one of her treasures and walked over to Sigrún, placing it gently in her lap. Sigrún's face lit up with joy, and she hugged her sister tightly, her small arms wrapping around Lóa.

Lóa smiled, feeling lighter than she ever had before. She hadn't lost anything—instead, she had gained something far more precious.

Askasleikir watched the scene unfold, satisfied with the change in Lóa's heart. "Well done," he said quietly.

"You've learned the power of sharing."

He turned to leave, his long arms swinging by his sides as he slipped back toward the door. But before disappearing into the night, he looked over his shoulder, his crooked grin returning. "Remember, Lóa," he said, "the more you give, the more you'll find waiting for you in return."

*Whoosh!*

The door closed behind him, and the cold wind blew through the house, though this time it carried a warmth that hadn't been there before.

Lóa sat by the fire with her brother and sister, her heart full of joy. She had discovered something more valuable than all her treasures—the happiness that came from sharing.

# Chapter 10: The Struggle Within Grýla

*Thud. Thud. Thud!*

Grýla's heavy boots pounded against the stone floor of her cave as she paced back and forth, her mind racing. The cold wind howled outside, but it was nothing compared to the storm of frustration brewing inside her. For centuries, she had ruled over the children of Iceland with fear, her Naughty List growing longer each Yule. And now? Now it was shrinking, disappearing before her eyes.

Her sons were behind this. She was certain of it. They had been meddling, helping children escape their rightful place on her list. And it infuriated her.

*Crash!*

Grýla swept her arm across the table, sending a pile of old bowls and spoons clattering to the floor. Her eyes blazed as she stormed to the entrance of her cave, staring out into the endless winter night.

*Whooooosh!*

The wind gusted around her, pulling at her cloak, but she barely noticed. Her thoughts were consumed by a growing sense of unease—something she hadn't felt in centuries. Fear and anger had always been her tools, her way of controlling the children and ensuring they behaved. But now, with her sons turning to kindness and second chances, she was losing her grip on the old ways.

Grýla growled, her hands clenching into fists. "What do they think they're doing?" she muttered to herself. "Helping the children? Kindness? It's nonsense. They'll never learn that way. Fear is what keeps them in line."

But even as she spoke the words, something inside her twisted uncomfortably. A small, long-forgotten voice whispered in the back of her mind, questioning everything she had believed for so long.

Had fear really worked all these years? Or had it simply kept children from understanding why they should be good, only making them afraid of the consequences?

Grýla shook her head violently, as if trying to rid herself of the thought. "No," she growled. "Fear has always worked. It's the way things have to be."

But deep down, she wasn't so sure anymore.

*Thump, thump, thump!*

She began pacing again, her mind flickering back to her own childhood, a time long ago, before her heart had turned cold. She had once been a young girl living in the village with her parents, helping them during the long winters. Back then, she had known warmth, kindness, and the joy of helping others. But life had hardened her, and over the centuries, she had become something… else.

Her memories of that time were blurry, like a dream she couldn't quite recall. But one thing stood out—there had been a time when she had believed in second chances.

When she had known that children could change not through fear, but through love and guidance.

Grýla stopped pacing, her hands trembling slightly. She hadn't thought about that in years. She had pushed it away, buried it deep beneath the layers of ice and snow that had formed around her heart.

*Clink!*

The sound of a small object hitting the floor broke the silence, and Grýla looked down to see one of the old bowls she had knocked over earlier. It rolled slowly across the floor, coming to rest against her boot. She stared at it, her mind whirling.

The Yule Lads—her sons—were doing what she had once known deep down was possible. They were giving children the chance to change, not through fear, but through lessons of kindness, honesty, and sharing.

Grýla bent down, picking up the bowl in her large hands. Her fingers traced the worn, rough surface, and for a moment, she could almost feel the warmth of a hearth fire, hear the laughter of children, and remember the joy of Yule as it had been in her childhood.

A memory surfaced—one she had long forgotten. She had been no different than the children on her Naughty List now. When she was young, she had made her share of mistakes, had been selfish and naughty at times. But someone had given her a second chance. Someone had shown her kindness.

Her mother.

Grýla clenched the bowl tightly, her breath catching in her throat. Her mother had always believed in her, even when she had misbehaved. She had taught Grýla the importance of forgiveness and understanding, of giving others the chance to make things right.

But over the years, Grýla had forgotten those lessons. She had let bitterness and anger consume her, turning her into the fearsome creature she had become. The Yule Lads had learned what she had lost, and now they were trying to show her the way back.

"No," Grýla muttered, her voice wavering. "I don't need second chances. I don't need kindness."

But the more she said it, the less she believed it. Her sons had seen something she hadn't—something she had been too stubborn to acknowledge. Maybe children didn't need to fear her. Maybe they could change on their own, with the right guidance.

Grýla's hands shook as she placed the bowl back on the table, her heart heavy with confusion. She had spent so many years building her reputation as the terrifying Yule ogress, punishing those who strayed. How could she let that go? Could she even change after all this time?

*Clunk, clunk, clunk!*

Grýla walked to the mouth of her cave, staring out into the cold, endless night. The wind had quieted, and the village lights twinkled far below in the valley, like stars on the earth. She could hear the faint sound of laughter on the breeze—children, happy and safe in their homes, unaware of the storm brewing in her heart.

A part of her wanted to cling to the old ways, to continue punishing the naughty and ruling through fear. It was familiar, and it had worked for so long. But another part of her, the part she had buried long ago, whispered of something different—something softer and warmer. Something she had lost, but could still find again.

Grýla took a deep breath, the cold air filling her lungs. She wasn't ready to give in just yet. The struggle within her was real, and it wasn't something she could solve in a single night. But for the first time in centuries, she began to wonder if maybe, just maybe, her sons were right.

Maybe there was another way to guide the children of Iceland. Maybe Yule was about more than fear and punishment.

Maybe even Grýla herself wasn't beyond a second chance.

## Chapter 11: Skyrgámur's Fairness Feast

*Gurgle, gurgle, gurgle.*

The sound of a rumbling stomach echoed through the small cottage as Snorri sat at the table, eyeing the large bowl of skyr in front of him. It was thick and creamy, his favorite treat, and he had been looking forward to this all day. But as usual, Snorri wasn't planning to share.

His younger sister, Freyja, sat across from him, her eyes wide as she watched him dig into the bowl, the spoon clinking against the side. She glanced over at their mother, who was busy tending to the fire, and then back at Snorri.

"Snorri, can I have some?" Freyja asked quietly, her voice hopeful.

Snorri didn't even look up. "No," he said sharply, shoveling another spoonful into his mouth. "It's mine. Get your own."

Freyja's face fell, and she looked down at her empty bowl, too shy to ask again. Their mother didn't notice the exchange, but Skyrgámur, the Yule Lad known for stealing skyr, had been watching.

*Plop, plop, plop!*

The Yule Lad's heavy boots moved quietly as he crouched by the window, his sharp eyes glinting in the soft light from the hearth. Skyrgámur's mouth watered at the sight

of the creamy skyr, but tonight he wasn't here to steal
t. No, tonight his mission was different. He had been
sent to teach Snorri a lesson—not about food, but about
fairness.

Skyrgámur's long, gangly frame slipped through the
back door, which creaked softly as he entered. Creeeak.
Neither Snorri nor Freyja noticed him at first, but
Skyrgámur wasn't one to go unnoticed for long.

Clunk! He knocked over a small wooden cup, causing
both children to jump. Snorri's spoon clattered into the
bowl as he looked up, his heart racing. "Who's there?" he
asked, his voice wavering.

Skyrgámur stepped forward, his crooked grin revealing
a set of sharp teeth. "It's me," he said, his voice low and
playful. "Skyrgámur, at your service."

Snorri's eyes widened in fear, and he quickly pulled the
bowl of skyr closer to himself. "You can't have it!" he
blurted out. "It's mine!"

Skyrgámur raised an eyebrow, his grin widening. "I wasn't
asking for it," he said, his voice filled with amusement.
"But it seems you're quite protective of it, aren't you?"

Snorri clutched the bowl even tighter, his face flushed.
"It's my favorite. I'm not sharing."

Skyrgámur crossed his arms, his eyes narrowing as he
regarded the boy. "I see," he said slowly. "And what
about your sister? Is it fair that you have all the skyr while

she sits there with an empty bowl?"

Snorri glanced at Freyja, who was watching him with wide, pleading eyes, but he quickly looked away. "It's not my fault she didn't get any," he muttered. "She can get her own."

Skyrgámur's grin faded slightly, and he stepped closer to the table. Thud, thud. His boots hit the floor with heavy steps, and Snorri shrank back in his chair. "Let me tell you something about fairness, Snorri," the Yule Lad said, his voice low but firm. "Yule is a time for sharing, for being fair to those around you. When you take more than your share, you leave others with nothing. Is that how you want to be remembered?"

Snorri blinked, his heart pounding in his chest. He hadn't thought about it that way. He had always just taken what he wanted, never really considering how it affected others. But now, with Skyrgámur standing over him, his sharp eyes fixed on Snorri's every move, the boy began to feel a pang of guilt.

"I... I didn't mean to take it all," Snorri said quietly, looking down at the bowl of skyr in his hands.

Skyrgámur nodded, his expression softening. "That may be true," he said. "But you did. And now, you have a chance to make things right."

Snorri glanced at Freyja again. She wasn't saying anything, but her eyes were filled with hope. He swallowed hard, feeling a strange tightness in his chest. "I guess I could share," he muttered, though the words elt heavy on his tongue.

Skyrgámur's grin returned, and he clapped his hands together. "That's more like it!" he said, his voice booming with approval. "Go on, then. Fill your sister's bowl."

Snorri hesitated for a moment, then slowly scooped a large spoonful of skyr into Freyja's empty bowl. The soft plop of the skyr hitting the wood was followed by a small gasp from Freyja. She looked up at her brother, her face lighting up with surprise and gratitude.

"Thank you, Snorri!" she said, her voice filled with joy.

Snorri didn't say anything, but he felt a warmth spreading in his chest, different from the usual satisfaction he got from keeping things to himself. He had never realized how happy it could make someone else to receive something, even if it meant having a little less for himself.

Skyrgámur nodded approvingly, his sharp teeth gleaming in the firelight. "Fairness isn't just about what you get," he said. "It's about making sure others have enough too. When you share what you have, you create balance. And that, my boy, is the spirit of Yule."

Snorri looked down at his own bowl, which still had plenty of skyr in it. He had given some away, but there was more than enough left for him. He smiled a little, realizing that he hadn't lost anything by sharing. In fact, he felt like he had gained something—something more important than the skyr itself.

Freyja took a bite of her skyr, her face glowing with happiness. "It's delicious!" she said, her voice full of excitement.

Snorri couldn't help but smile back at her. "Yeah," he said, taking a spoonful for himself. "It is."

Skyrgámur chuckled softly, watching the siblings enjoy their shared meal. "You've learned an important lesson tonight, Snorri," he said. "Fairness isn't just about taking what you want. It's about making sure everyone has enough. And when you do that, you'll find that there's more to go around than you thought."

Snorri nodded, his heart lighter than it had been in a long time. "I think I get it now," he said softly.

Skyrgámur grinned, his sharp teeth gleaming once more. "Good. Remember that, boy. Fairness brings more than just full bellies—it brings peace to the heart."

With that, the Yule Lad turned and headed for the door. But before he left, he glanced over his shoulder, his eyes twinkling with mischief. "And Snorri," he said with a sly grin, "next time you have a bowl of skyr, don't be surprised if I come sniffing around. Old habits die hard, after all."

Whoosh! The door swung open, and Skyrgámur disappeared into the cold night, leaving behind the warmth of the small cottage.

Snorri sat back in his chair, feeling a sense of calm settle over him. He glanced at Freyja, who was happily finishing her skyr, and smiled. Sharing hadn't been as hard as he thought it would be. In fact, it felt… good.

"Do you want some more?" Snorri asked, holding out the spoon.

Freyja's face lit up with surprise. "Really?"

Snorri nodded. "Yeah. There's enough for both of us."

As they finished their meal together, the warmth of Yule filled the cottage, not just from the fire, but from the simple act of fairness and the joy of sharing.

# Chapter 12: Grýla's Storm

*Whooooooosh!*

The wind howled furiously through the mountains, the icy cold biting at the rocks like sharp teeth. Snow swirled in violent gusts as Grýla stood at the entrance of her cave, her heart heavy with frustration. Her sons—her own sons—had turned against her. Instead of keeping children in line through fear, they were helping them. Teaching them lessons of kindness and fairness, guiding them away from the Naughty List she had kept for centuries.

Grýla's hands clenched into fists as the storm inside her grew stronger. She had tried to shake off the nagging doubts, to ignore the whispers of change, but it was no use. Her Naughty List had continued to shrink, and the Yule Lads had openly defied her, giving children second chances she didn't believe they deserved.

*Thump, thump, thump!*

Grýla's heavy boots echoed through the cave as she paced, her mind swirling with anger. "They think they can change things," she muttered to herself, her voice low and dangerous. "But they forget who I am. They forget what Yule is really about."

Her dark eyes flashed as she stared out into the blizzard, the storm mirroring the tempest inside her. She had watched for too long, letting her sons interfere with her work. Now, it was time to remind them—and the children of Iceland—who held the true power during Yule.

*Thud, thwaaack, crack!*

With a mighty swing of her arm, Grýla knocked over her cauldron, sending it clattering across the cave floor. Sparks from the fire hissed and popped as they hit the cold stone, and the snow outside seemed to howl even louder, as if the storm itself answered her rage.

"They've gone soft," Grýla growled. "Yule is about consequences, about keeping the children in line. If they don't fear me, how will they ever learn?"

But even as she spoke, that small, nagging voice inside her whispered again. Was fear really the only way? Couldn't children learn without being afraid? Grýla shook her head, trying to banish the thought. No. Fear had always worked. It had to.

Grýla stormed to the back of her cave, her heart pounding in her chest. She wasn't going to stand by and let her sons change everything she had built. If they wanted to show kindness, she would remind them—and the children—why the old ways mattered. And she would do it her way.

*Thump, thump, thump!*

Grýla's boots struck the ground with purpose as she headed toward a large stone chest hidden deep in the shadows of her cave. Her hands shook with barely contained fury as she reached for the iron latch. This chest held something powerful—something she hadn't used in many years.

Inside was her most dangerous tool: the power to control the very elements of Yule itself.

*Click!*

The latch snapped open, and Grýla flung the chest wide. Inside, nestled among old furs and trinkets, was a simple wooden staff. It didn't look like much, but Grýla knew its power well. With it, she could summon storms—real storms—blizzards strong enough to blanket the land and trap her sons before they could finish their "missions" of kindness.

Grýla grabbed the staff and held it tightly in her hands, her eyes narrowing as she strode back toward the entrance of the cave. She could already feel the magic stirring within the wood, the cold power seeping into her bones.

Outside, the storm was already fierce, but Grýla wasn't finished. She raised the staff high, her voice booming into the night. "If my sons want to play the part of heroes, let's see how they fare against this."

With a sharp twist of her wrist, she slammed the staff into the ground. The earth beneath her feet trembled, and the wind roared in response. Whoooooooosh! The snow picked up speed, swirling into a blinding blizzard that stretched far and wide, covering the village below in a thick, icy blanket.

*CRASH!*

Lightning flashed in the sky, followed by a deafening crack of thunder. The air grew colder, the snow falling faster and harder. Grýla stood at the mouth of the cave, watching as her storm spread across the land. The children would feel her presence tonight—there would be no more second chances, no more softness. Her sons wouldn't be able to finish their work. They wouldn't be able to help the children.

"They've forgotten who I am," Grýla muttered darkly. "But they'll remember now."

As the storm raged on, she thought of the Yule Lads, scattered across the villages, trying to finish their "missions" of kindness. They had been so certain that second chances could change the children, but Grýla knew better. She had seen too much, lived through too many winters. Fear was what kept people in line, not hope.

But as the snow continued to fall, burying the village under a thick white blanket, a small voice inside her whispered again. Was she truly doing this for the children—or for herself? Was her anger at her sons' new path really because she believed they were wrong? Or was it because she was afraid?

Afraid? Grýla scoffed at the thought. She wasn't afraid of anything. But still, the whisper wouldn't go away.

Was she afraid that without fear, the children wouldn't need her anymore? That without her, Yule would move on without the old ways, without the Naughty List? And if the Naughty List disappeared… what would be left for

Grýla?

The storm raged around her, the wind howling like wolves in the night. Whoooooooosh! But even as she stood there, watching the snow pile higher and higher, doubt crept into her heart.

Her sons had found a new way, one that didn't rely on fear. They were teaching children to change, to be better, without threatening them. They were giving second chances. And though Grýla had fought it, though she had clung to her old ways with all her might, part of her wondered if maybe... just maybe... they were right.

The staff in her hand felt heavier than before, the cold seeping deeper into her skin. For centuries, she had believed that she had to be feared. That without fear, there was no Yule, no balance, no reason for her. But now, as the snowstorm raged, she couldn't help but wonder if there was another way.

Grýla clenched her jaw, her eyes narrowing as she looked out over the frozen landscape. "No," she whispered to herself. "This is how it's always been."

But the storm felt different this time. It didn't feel like power. It felt like something else—something colder, lonelier.

Grýla stood still, the snow swirling around her, as the struggle within her heart deepened. The storm outside might have been fierce, but the storm inside her was even stronger.

# Chapter 13: The Yule Lads Unite

*Whoooooooosh!*

The storm raged through the mountains and valleys, snow swirling and piling up higher by the minute. The wind howled like a pack of wolves, the bitter cold biting at anything and anyone caught in its path. It was a blizzard like none the Yule Lads had seen before, and they knew exactly who was behind it. Grýla!

*Crunch, crunch, crunch!*

Stekkjastaur trudged through the deep snow, his stiff legs barely able to move in the thick drifts. His breath came in ragged puffs, but he didn't stop. He couldn't. There were still children who needed his help. But the storm—this storm wasn't natural. It was Grýla's doing, a reminder of her power.

Clomp, clomp. He forced his way through the snow, his eyes scanning the distance. He had to find his brothers. They couldn't finish their missions alone—not in this weather.

"Giljagaur!" Stekkjastaur called out into the storm, his voice barely carrying over the howling wind. "Stúfur!"

The snow pelted his face, and he narrowed his eyes against the wind. He knew his brothers were out there, somewhere, trying to help the children before Grýla's storm stopped them. But they wouldn't be able to finish their work if they didn't band together.

Crunch, crunch. Stekkjastaur pushed forward, his legs aching with each step. Finally, through the thick wall of snow, he spotted a dark shape moving toward him.

"Stekkjastaur!" The voice was familiar. It was Giljagaur, his brother, plowing through the snow with a look of grim determination on his face.

Stekkjastaur breathed a sigh of relief. "Giljagaur! Thank the stars, I found you."

Giljagaur nodded, his face pale from the cold but his eyes fierce. "It's Grýla's storm," he said, his voice low. "She knows what we're doing, and she's trying to stop us."

Stekkjastaur clenched his fists. "We can't let her. The children need us. We have to finish what we started."

Giljagaur nodded in agreement, but before either of them could say more, another figure appeared through the swirling snow. It was Stúfur, the smallest of the brothers, nearly buried in the snowdrifts as he fought to reach them.

"Stekkjastaur! Giljagaur!" Stúfur called, his voice barely audible over the wind. "We have to get through this storm. There are still children who need our help."

The three brothers huddled together, the snow whipping around them like a living thing. The storm was getting worse, and they knew that if they didn't find a way to stop it, all their efforts to help the children would be lost.

"We need the others," Stekkjastaur said firmly. "We can't face this storm alone. If we're going to finish what we started, we need every Yule Lad."

Giljagaur nodded, his face set with determination. "I saw Þvörusleikir heading toward the village earlier. He's probably still out there. Let's find him and the rest."

The Yule Lads set off together, their figures barely visible in the blinding snow. The wind roared around them, but they pressed on, driven by a single purpose: to unite and stand against their mother's storm.

*Clomp, clomp, clomp!*

Their stiff boots crunched through the deep snow as they made their way toward the village. It wasn't long before they found Þvörusleikir, his long arms wrapped around himself to keep warm, his spoon tucked under one arm as he fought against the blizzard.

"Þvörusleikir!" Giljagaur called out. "Over here!"

The tall, lanky Yule Lad turned, his sharp eyes narrowing against the wind. "What in the name of Yule is happening?" he shouted as they reached him. "This storm—it's not natural."

"It's Grýla," Stekkjastaur said grimly. "She's trying to stop us from helping the children. We have to get through this storm together."

Þvörusleikir's eyes darkened. "So, she knows what we've

been doing." He gripped his spoon tightly. "I should have known."

One by one, they found the rest of the Yule Lads— Askasleikir, Skyrgámur, Kertasníkir, and the others— scattered across the village, each of them struggling against the storm but refusing to give up. They gathered under the shelter of a large tree, huddled together as the snow continued to fall in thick, swirling sheets.

"We can't let Grýla stop us," Stúfur said, his voice shaking with cold but filled with determination. "The children are counting on us."

"But how are we supposed to finish our work in this?" Askasleikir asked, glancing up at the blizzard that showed no signs of letting up. "We can barely move through the snow, let alone help the children."

Stekkjastaur thought for a moment, his mind racing. "We can't fight this storm with force," he said slowly. "But we can work together. Each of us has something we bring to the table. We can use our strengths to get through this."

The Yule Lads exchanged glances, nodding slowly as they realized what Stekkjastaur meant. They had spent centuries relying on their mischief, each of them working alone, but this was different. This time, they had to unite, not just as tricksters, but as brothers with a common goal.

"We can't stop the storm," Giljagaur said, "but we can outlast it. We'll finish our missions, no matter what Grýla throws at us."

74

Kertasníkir, the Candle Stealer, nodded, his face determined. "We'll bring light to the children, even in this storm. They need hope, and we can give it to them."

One by one, the Yule Lads came together, each offering their unique talents to help the children through the blizzard. Stúfur, with his small size, slipped through narrow passageways to deliver help to families snowed in. Þvörusleikir and Askasleikir used their long arms to clear paths through the snow, and Skyrgámur shared what food he could find with those in need.

Together, they braved the storm, working as a team to finish what they had started. The wind roared around them, but their spirits were strong. They weren't just tricksters anymore—they were something more.

As the night wore on, the storm began to weaken, its strength no longer able to overpower the unity of the Yule Lads. Grýla's fury might have been fierce, but the bond between the brothers—and their mission to help the children—was stronger.

*Whoooooosh!*

The wind began to die down, the snow falling more gently now, blanketing the village in a soft, peaceful white.

The Yule Lads stood together at the edge of the village, their work finally complete. They had made it through the storm, not because of mischief, but because of their newfound purpose.

Stekkjastaur looked around at his brothers, pride swelling in his chest. "We did it," he said quietly.

Giljagaur grinned. "Grýla's storm couldn't stop us."

Kertasníkir held up a small, flickering candle, its warm light glowing in the darkness. "Hope is stronger than fear," he said softly.

The Yule Lads stood together, united in a way they had never been before. They had found a new path, one that didn't rely on fear or tricks. And though the storm had tested them, they had come out stronger—together.

# Chapter 14: Kertasníkir's Candle of Hope

*Flicker, flicker, flicker.*

The soft flame of a single candle danced in the wind as Kertasníkir, the Candle Stealer, made his way through the quiet village. Snow still blanketed the ground from Grýla's storm, but the fierce winds had died down, leaving the night eerily calm. Kertasníkir moved quietly, the small light in his hands casting a gentle glow against the dark shadows of the houses.

He had a special task tonight, one that weighed heavy on his heart. Of all the Yule Lads, Kertasníkir understood the importance of light in the darkness. He had always loved candles, sneaking into homes to steal their glowing warmth, but this year was different. This year, he wasn't taking candles—he was giving them.

*Crunch, crunch, crunch!*

His boots sank into the fresh snow as he approached a small cottage at the edge of the village. The windows were dark, and the house looked cold and lonely, almost as though it had been forgotten. Kertasníkir knew it wasn't empty, though. Inside lived a girl named Birta, and she was in need of something only he could bring: hope.

Birta had lost much over the past year. Her father had fallen ill, and her mother was working day and night to provide for the family. With Yule approaching, Birta had grown quieter, more withdrawn, her heart heavy with sadness. She had given up hope that this Yule could be merry. She no longer looked forward to the magic of the season, and the weight of the dark winter had settled over her like a heavy blanket.

Kertasníkir had heard about Birta, and as he stood outside her cottage, he knew his mission. He had to bring her a light—a candle to reignite her hope.

Tap, tap. He knocked gently on the door, but there was no answer. Birta's mother had likely gone to the village market, and Birta herself was probably inside, too sad to answer the door.

With a gentle push, Kertasníkir opened the door, the soft creak barely audible over the stillness of the night. Inside, the cottage was dim, with only the faintest glow from the dying embers in the hearth. Birta sat by the fire, her knees pulled up to her chest, her eyes distant as she stared at the flickering light.

Kertasníkir stepped inside, the warmth of the small candle in his hands a stark contrast to the cold air in the room. He moved silently, his long frame slipping through the shadows until he stood beside Birta. She didn't notice him at first, her thoughts far away, lost in the sorrow that weighed on her heart.

"Birta," Kertasníkir said softly, his voice like a whisper in the dark.

The girl blinked, startled by the sound, and looked up. Her eyes widened as she saw the tall figure of the Yule Lad standing next to her, his sharp features illuminated by the small candle in his hands.

"Who… who are you?" she asked, her voice small and uncertain.

Kertasníkir smiled gently. "I'm Kertasníkir," he said. "But you don't need to be afraid. I'm not here to steal your candles tonight. I'm here to give you one."

Birta frowned, confused. "Give me a candle? Why?"

Kertasníkir knelt beside her, holding the flickering flame in front of her. "Because you've lost your light, Birta," he said quietly. "Yule is a time of warmth, of hope, but you've forgotten that. You've let the darkness take over, and you've given up. This candle," he said, his voice soft and steady, "is a reminder that even in the darkest times, there is still light."

Birta's eyes filled with tears as she looked at the small flame, its soft glow reflecting in her dark, tired eyes. "But everything feels so… hopeless," she whispered. "Yule is supposed to be a happy time, but I can't feel it. Not this year."

Kertasníkir's heart ached as he listened to her words. He knew how easily the darkness could settle in during the long winter nights, how quickly hope could fade when things seemed bleak. But he also knew that even the smallest light could make a difference.

He gently placed the candle on the table in front of her, its warm glow filling the room with a soft, comforting light. "You're not alone, Birta," he said. "Even when it feels like everything is dark, there are still people who care about you. Your mother, your friends… they haven't forgotten you."

Birta sniffled, wiping her eyes with the sleeve of her sweater. "But it's so hard," she said, her voice trembling. "Everything feels so heavy, and I don't know how to make it better."

Kertasníkir nodded, understanding. "Sometimes, we can't fix everything all at once," he said gently. "But we can take small steps, little by little. And sometimes, all it takes is a tiny light to remind us that things can get better."

Birta stared at the candle, the warmth from the flame spreading through the room. She felt something stir inside her, a small flicker of hope that had been buried deep beneath her sadness. It wasn't much, but it was enough to remind her that she wasn't alone—that even in the darkest times, there could be light.

"Yule isn't just about the gifts and the feasts," Kertasníkir continued softly. "It's about hope. It's about the promise that the darkness won't last forever. And this candle," he said, gesturing to the small flame, "is your reminder of that."

Birta took a deep breath, her heart feeling just a little lighter as she gazed at the candle. "Do you really think things will get better?" she asked, her voice barely above a whisper.

Kertasníkir smiled. "I know they will," he said. "And when the darkness feels too much, just remember that the light is always there, even if it's small. Hope doesn't have to be big to be powerful."

Birta nodded slowly, her tears drying as she allowed herself to believe, even just a little, that things could change. She reached out and gently touched the base of the candle, feeling the warmth of the flame seep into her fingers.

"Thank you," she whispered, her voice filled with gratitude.

Kertasníkir stood up, his heart full as he watched the light begin to return to Birta's eyes. "Take care of that candle," he said. "And remember, the light you carry inside you is just as important as the one you hold in your hands."

Birta smiled, a real, genuine smile that hadn't touched her face in weeks. "I will."

With that, Kertasníkir turned to leave, his mission complete. As he reached the door, he glanced back at the small, glowing candle on the table. The room seemed warmer now, filled with the soft glow of hope that would guide Birta through the dark days ahead.

*Whoosh!*

The door closed gently behind him as Kertasníkir stepped back into the cold night, the storm long gone, leaving the village quiet and peaceful once more.

The stars twinkled above, and Kertasníkir felt a sense of calm settle over him. He had done more than deliver a candle tonight. He had helped someone find their hope again.

And as he disappeared into the shadows, he knew that even the smallest light could make all the difference in the world.

# Chapter 15: Grýla's Final Test

Whoooooosh. The storm had passed, but the winds of change still whispered through the mountains. Grýla stood at the mouth of her cave, staring out over the snow-covered village below. The blizzard she had unleashed had been fierce, but it hadn't stopped the Yule Lads. Somehow, despite the storm, they had finished their work. They had helped the children.

Her sons had defied her.

Grýla's fists clenched at her sides, her black cloak billowing around her as she stepped outside. She could feel the frustration boiling inside her. She had been certain that fear was the way—the only way—to teach the children of Iceland to behave. But her sons had chosen a different path, one she didn't understand.

Thump, thump, thump. Grýla's heavy boots crunched through the snow as she made her way down the mountain, toward the village. She could feel the fire of her anger burning in her chest, but alongside it was something else—something unfamiliar and unsettling.

Doubt.

For the first time in centuries, Grýla wasn't sure of herself. The Yule Lads had accomplished something she had never imagined possible. They had changed the hearts of children not through fear, but through kindness. And the Naughty List had shrunk because of it.

Was it possible she had been wrong all this time?

Crunch, crunch. Grýla's boots sank deeper into the snow as she approached the edge of the village. The lights in the windows twinkled softly, and she could hear the faint sound of laughter from inside the homes. Children's laughter. It was a sound she wasn't used to hearing at this time of year.

Her sons had succeeded in their mission, and Grýla had a choice to make.

Thud, thud. Her footsteps grew heavier as she approached a small clearing at the center of the village. She could see the Yule Lads gathered there, standing together beneath a large tree. They hadn't noticed her yet, but Grýla's presence was impossible to ignore for long.

Stekkjastaur was the first to spot her. His stiff-legged stance froze as he turned to face his mother, his eyes wide with a mixture of surprise and determination.

"Mother," he said, his voice steady despite the fear in his chest. The other Yule Lads turned, each of them tensing as Grýla stepped into the clearing.

Grýla's dark eyes scanned her sons, her jaw tight. They had defied her, gone against everything she had taught them. But as she looked at them—Stekkjastaur, Giljagaur, Stúfur, and the rest—she didn't see rebellion. She saw something else. They weren't standing in defiance. They were standing together, united by something stronger than fear.

84

"Why?" Grýla growled, her voice low and dangerous. "Why have you turned against me?"

Stekkjastaur took a step forward, his stiff legs crunching through the snow. "We haven't turned against you, Mother," he said quietly. "We've just... found a new way."

Grýla's eyes narrowed. "A new way? By defying everything I've taught you? By ignoring the Naughty List?"

"We haven't ignored it," Giljagaur said, stepping up beside his brother. "We've helped children get off the list. We've shown them that they can change, not through fear, but through second chances."

Grýla's fists tightened, her anger bubbling to the surface. "Second chances," she spat. "Do you think they'll learn anything without consequences? Do you think they'll behave if they don't fear what happens when they don't?"

"They've already learned," Stúfur said, his small voice rising above the wind. "They've learned because we've taught them. We've given them the chance to be better, to make up for their mistakes."

Grýla's heart pounded in her chest, her thoughts swirling with confusion. She had raised her sons to be tricksters, to use fear to keep the children in line. But now, as she looked at them, standing together, united in their belief in second chances, she began to wonder if fear had ever been enough.

"They fear me," she said, her voice quieter now, almost uncertain. "That's how it's always been."

"Maybe that's the problem," said Giljagaur gently. "Maybe fear isn't what they need anymore. Maybe it never was."

Grýla blinked, her heart racing. For so long, she had believed that her role in Yule was to be feared. She had held onto that belief with everything she had, convinced that without her, the children would misbehave and chaos would reign. But now, as she looked at her sons, she wasn't so sure.

"Fear has kept them in line," she muttered, more to herself than to her sons. "Fear has always worked."

"But it's not working anymore," Stekkjastaur said, his voice soft but firm. "The children aren't learning through fear, Mother. They're learning through kindness, through second chances. They're learning that they can be better, not because they're afraid of you, but because they want to be."

Grýla stared at her sons, her heart heavy with conflict. They had chosen a different path, and it was working. The children were changing, and the Naughty List was shrinking. But that left Grýla with a question she had been avoiding for far too long: What was her place now?

For centuries, she had ruled Yule with fear, but if fear was no longer needed... what would become of her?

"What am I supposed to do now?" Grýla asked, her voice barely a whisper. "If the children don't fear me... what am I?"

The Yule Lads exchanged glances, unsure how to answer their mother. They had never seen her like this—so vulnerable, so uncertain. It was as if the storm inside her had broken, and all that was left was a woman who didn't know where she fit in the world anymore.

"Maybe you don't need to be feared anymore," Stúfur said gently, stepping forward. "Maybe you can help, too. You could teach the children, like we have."

Grýla's eyes widened in surprise. "Teach them?"

Stekkjastaur nodded. "You've seen more Yules than any of us, Mother. You know the traditions, the stories, the lessons. You don't have to be feared to be respected. You could help guide them, show them what Yule is really about."

Grýla's heart pounded as she took in her sons' words. Could she change? Could she, the fearsome Grýla, become something different? Something better?

The wind blew softly through the clearing, carrying with it the scent of pine and snow. Grýla closed her eyes for a moment, feeling the weight of centuries lift from her shoulders. It wasn't an easy decision. It wasn't something she could do overnight. But maybe, just maybe, her sons were right.

Maybe even Grýla deserved a second chance.

When she opened her eyes, the storm inside her had quieted. She looked at her sons, her voice steadier now. "If I do this," she said slowly, "if I change… will they accept me?"

"They will," Stekkjastaur said softly. "But only if you give them the chance."

Grýla nodded, her heart still heavy, but lighter than it had been in centuries. "Then maybe it's time I gave them that chance."

The Yule Lads smiled, relief and hope in their eyes. They had faced their mother's fury and won—not through defiance, but through love.

Grýla stood tall, the storm around her fading as she faced her final test. The children of Iceland no longer needed to fear her, but that didn't mean her place in Yule was gone. It was simply… changing.

And for the first time in a very long time, Grýla was ready to change, too.

# Chapter 16: Grýla's Transformation

*Whoooooosh!*

The wind had settled into a soft breeze, whispering through the trees and across the snow-covered hills as Grýla stood in the quiet village, surrounded by her sons. The storm, both outside and within, had passed, leaving only stillness behind. Grýla's dark eyes, once filled with fury and defiance, now reflected a different kind of storm—a quiet struggle, a realization that the old ways no longer fit the world around her.

The Yule Lads watched their mother in silence, unsure of what would happen next. Grýla had spent centuries being the terror of Yule, the one who punished the naughty, but now the world was changing. They had changed. And for the first time, Grýla was beginning to understand that maybe she could change, too.

Stekkjastaur stepped forward, his voice gentle. "Mother, you don't have to let go of everything," he said. "You don't have to be feared to have a place in Yule."

Grýla looked at him, her expression unreadable. "And what place is there for me if I am not feared?" she asked softly.

Giljagaur, standing beside his brother, took a deep breath. "You know more about Yule than anyone else, Mother. You could guide the children, teach them the lessons of Yule without the fear."

Grýla's heart felt heavy as she listened to her sons. It was true—she had lived through more Yules than anyone could count, seen the traditions and stories evolve through the centuries. But for so long, her role had been one of fear, of punishment. Could she really become something different?

*Thump, thump, thump!*

Her boots echoed on the snow as she paced slowly, her thoughts swirling like the snowflakes drifting down from the sky. She thought back to her childhood, before she had become the fearsome figure she was now. She had been just like the children on her Naughty List— misbehaving, making mistakes. But her mother had believed in her, given her second chances. That was a time before fear had hardened her heart.

Maybe now was the time to remember those lessons. Maybe it was time to stop clinging to the past and embrace a future where she didn't have to be feared.

Grýla stopped pacing, her gaze drifting toward the village. In the distance, she could see children playing in the snow, their laughter ringing through the air. They didn't fear her now. They didn't even know she was there. And as she watched them, something strange happened inside her—something warm.

The children were happy, not because they were afraid of her, but because they had learned kindness, honesty, and sharing. They had learned the true meaning of Yule, and it hadn't come from fear.

Stekkjastaur stepped forward again, his voice quiet but firm. "You've always had the power to guide them, Mother," he said. "But now, you can guide them in a different way."

Grýla looked at him, her heart still heavy but softening. "I'm not sure I know how," she admitted, her voice uncharacteristically quiet. "I've been feared for so long… I don't know how to be anything else."

Giljagaur smiled softly. "It won't happen all at once. But you don't have to do it alone. We'll be here to help."

The other Yule Lads nodded in agreement, their eyes filled with hope. They had seen their mother's struggle, and now, they saw the first flicker of change in her.

Grýla took a deep breath, the cold winter air filling her lungs. The weight of centuries of fear and punishment sat on her shoulders, but for the first time, she allowed herself to think that maybe it was a burden she didn't have to carry anymore.

"If I do this," she said slowly, "if I change… it won't be easy."

Stekkjastaur nodded. "Change never is," he said. "But it's worth it."

Grýla looked out at the village once more, watching as the children played in the snow, their laughter like music to her ears. She had always thought that the only way to control the children was through fear, but now, she was beginning to see that there was another way.

"I won't punish them anymore," she said quietly, more to herself than to her sons. "I won't make them afraid."

Giljagaur's eyes softened. "You don't have to. You can teach them."

Grýla stood in silence for a long moment, the snow falling softly around her. She had spent so long being feared, so long clinging to her role as the punisher of the naughty. But now, she could feel the coldness in her heart beginning to thaw.

Slowly, she turned to face her sons, her voice steady. "Then I will change," she said quietly. "But it won't be easy."

The Yule Lads smiled, their hearts swelling with relief and pride. "We'll help you, Mother," Stúfur said, his small voice filled with warmth. "We'll do it together."

Grýla nodded, though her heart was still heavy with uncertainty. She wasn't used to being soft, to showing kindness. But if her sons believed in her, maybe she could believe in herself, too.

Over the next few days, Grýla began her slow transformation. It wasn't easy, and it wasn't instant. She struggled with the temptation to fall back into her old ways. There were moments when she wanted to storm through the village, reminding the children of who she was, of what they should fear. But each time the urge grew too strong, one of her sons would be there, reminding her of their new mission—reminding her of the power of second chances.

Grýla had opened her cave to the children of the village, though they were hesitant at first. Word spread quickly that the old Yule ogress, the one they had feared for so long, was no longer the terrifying figure she once was. Slowly, children began to visit her cave, curious to see if the rumors were true.

At first, Grýla didn't know what to do with them. She wasn't used to speaking softly or offering guidance. But as the children gathered around her, wide-eyed and full of questions, something inside her began to shift.

She started telling them stories. Not stories of fear or punishment, but stories of Yule—tales of hope, of second chances, of the old traditions that had been forgotten. The children listened in awe, their faces glowing in the soft light of the fire. They weren't afraid of her anymore. They were learning from her.

The Yule Lads watched from the shadows, their hearts full as they saw their mother slowly embrace her new role. She was no longer the terrifying figure they had once known. She was becoming something more—something better.

One evening, as Grýla sat by the fire with a group of children at her feet, she realized that something had changed inside her. The coldness that had filled her heart for so long had melted away, replaced by a warmth she hadn't felt in centuries.

The children looked up at her, their eyes wide with curiosity and trust. They weren't afraid of her. They respected her. And for the first time in a very long time, Grýla felt at peace.

She smiled softly, her voice steady as she told them the story of the very first Yule. It was a story she hadn't told in centuries, one filled with hope, joy, and second chances.

As she spoke, the fire crackled softly, the warmth spreading through the cave and into her heart. Grýla had finally found her place in Yule—not as the ogress to be feared, but as a guide, a teacher.

Her transformation wasn't complete, but it had begun. And for the first time in centuries, Grýla felt like she truly belonged.

# Chapter 17: A New Yule Tradition

The village was quieter than usual, the soft glow of the evening sun reflecting off the fresh snow, casting a peaceful light over the rooftops. For as long as anyone could remember, the children of Iceland had feared Yule, their minds filled with stories of Grýla, the terrifying ogress who would take naughty children away. But this year, something had changed.

*Clink, clink, clink!*

The sound of laughter and clattering bowls filled Grýla's once dark and ominous cave, now transformed into a warm and welcoming place. Inside, the children of the village gathered around Grýla, their faces lit by the fire and the flicker of small candles, their eyes wide as they listened to her.

Grýla, who had spent centuries lurking in the shadows, was now seated by the hearth, her hands resting gently on her lap. Her voice was soft but steady, filled with the wisdom of countless Yules. She was telling the children the tale of a long-forgotten Yule tradition—one that celebrated kindness, growth, and second chances.

"The first Yule wasn't just about the gifts," Grýla explained, her eyes twinkling as she spoke. "It was about families coming together, about helping those who needed it most, and about the promise that everyone, no matter what, could be better."

The children leaned forward, eager to hear more. Grýla had once been a figure of fear, but now she was a storyteller, a teacher. The transformation that had begun within her was becoming a new tradition for the village—a Yule not centered on fear, but on love, growth, and redemption.

Outside the cave, the Yule Lads stood together, watching through the open entrance as Grýla shared her stories. They had played a role in bringing about this change, and now, they too were a part of this new Yule tradition.

"We did it," Stekkjastaur said quietly, his voice filled with pride. "We've changed things."

Giljagaur nodded. "It feels strange, doesn't it? But good."

The brothers had always been tricksters, causing mischief wherever they went, but this year had been different. They had given the children second chances, helped them learn important lessons, and in doing so, they had changed themselves as well. Now, they were no longer feared—they were welcomed.

As the evening wore on, more villagers arrived at the cave. Parents came to collect their children, but many stayed to listen to Grýla's stories themselves. They, too, had grown up with tales of the fearsome ogress, but now they saw her in a new light.

Tap, tap. Kertasníkir, the Candle Stealer, stepped inside the cave, holding a small candle in his hands. He approached Grýla and set the candle gently on the table beside her.

"For you, Mother," he said softly. "A light for the new Yule."

Grýla smiled, her heart full as she looked at the glowing flame. It had been centuries since she had felt this kind of warmth—not just from the fire, but from the people around her.

"Thank you," she said quietly, her voice thick with emotion.

As the cave filled with light and laughter, the villagers began to realize that this was the beginning of something new. A new Yule tradition was taking shape—one where Grýla was not feared, but respected as a wise guide, where the Yule Lads weren't tricksters, but helpers.

The following day, as Yule officially began, the village was buzzing with excitement. The Yule Lads had scattered throughout the town, continuing their work of spreading kindness and teaching the children important lessons. But this year, instead of sneaking in under the cover of darkness, they were welcomed with open arms.

Children eagerly awaited the arrival of the Yule Lads, not with fear, but with anticipation. Each Lad brought with him a new lesson, a new way to celebrate Yule. Stekkjastaur visited the farms, teaching the children how to care for the animals with compassion. Giljagaur shared stories about the importance of generosity, while Stúfur encouraged even the smallest children to help with chores.

The villagers had embraced this new tradition, where Yule

was no longer about fear of punishment, but about hope, learning, and the joy of coming together as a community.

In the evenings, families gathered in Grýla's cave to listen to her stories. The cave, once dark and foreboding, was now a place of warmth and light. Grýla's transformation was becoming part of the new Yule tradition. She wasn't just a figure of legend anymore—she was a living reminder of the power of second chances.

One evening, as the fire crackled softly and the children gathered around, Grýla told the tale of her own transformation. She spoke of the centuries she had spent punishing the naughty, of the belief she had once held that fear was the only way to teach children to behave. But then, she told them how her sons had shown her a different path—a path of kindness, forgiveness, and growth.

"I thought I had to be feared," Grýla said, her voice steady but full of emotion. "But now I see that fear isn't the answer. Love, understanding, and second chances— those are what change hearts."

The children listened intently, their faces glowing in the firelight. They hadn't known the Grýla of the past—they only knew the Grýla who had welcomed them into her cave, who had shared her wisdom with them. To them, she was no longer a figure of fear. She was a guide, a teacher, and a symbol of hope.

As Grýla finished her story, one of the children, a young boy named Einar, looked up at her with wide eyes. "Will you still have a Naughty List, Grýla?" he asked quietly.

Grýla smiled, her heart light. "I won't need one," she said. "Because I believe that every child has the chance to be good, no matter what mistakes they've made."

The room fell silent for a moment, and then the children burst into applause, their faces full of joy. Grýla felt a warmth spread through her chest. This—this—was what Yule was meant to be. Not a time of fear, but a time of growth, of learning, and of second chances.

And so, the new Yule tradition took root in the village. Every year, the children would visit Grýla's cave, not to be punished, but to learn. The Yule Lads became symbols of hope and redemption, their mischief transformed into lessons of kindness and generosity.

Grýla's cave became a place of stories, a gathering place for the village during the long winter nights. Parents and children alike would come to sit by the fire, to listen to the old tales of Yule, and to be reminded of the importance of second chances.

And as the years passed, the legend of Grýla and the Yule Lads changed. No longer were they feared—they were celebrated. The children of Iceland looked forward to Yule, not with dread, but with excitement, knowing that it was a time for growth, for learning, and for coming together as a community.

Grýla's transformation had become the heart of the new Yule tradition, and in doing so, she had found her place—not as a figure of fear, but as a guide, a mentor, and a symbol of the true spirit of Yule.

## Chapter 18: The Legacy of the Yule Lads

*Crunch, crunch, crunch!*

The snow crunched under the Yule Lads' boots as they walked through the village, their breath visible in the cold winter air. It was the last night of Yule, and the village was peaceful, wrapped in the warmth of the new traditions that had blossomed over the season. The stars twinkled overhead, their soft light casting a gentle glow over the snow-covered rooftops.

Stekkjastaur led the group, his stiff legs moving more easily now that his heart was lighter. Behind him walked Giljagaur, Stúfur, and the rest of the Yule Lads, their eyes bright as they reflected on the changes that had taken place. It had been a long journey, but they had done it. They had transformed Yule—not just for the children, but for themselves as well.

As they reached the center of the village, the brothers paused, gazing at the twinkling lights that adorned the homes. The village was quiet, the families inside gathered around their hearths, sharing stories, gifts, and laughter. The fear that had once shadowed Yule had melted away, replaced by warmth and joy.

"It's hard to believe," Stúfur said quietly, his small voice carrying through the still night. "We've come so far."

Giljagaur nodded, his face filled with pride. "We used to be tricksters, sneaking into homes, causing mischief, and making children afraid of Yule. But now…" He gestured toward the village, where the soft glow of candles flickered in every window. "Now, we're part of something bigger."

Stekkjastaur smiled, his heart full as he looked at his brothers. "It wasn't easy," he said, his voice thoughtful. "But it was worth it. We've changed, and because of that, Yule has changed too."

The Yule Lads stood in silence for a moment, each of them reflecting on the journey they had taken. It hadn't been simple—convincing their mother, Grýla, to let go of her old ways had been a challenge. But in the end, she had embraced the change, and now she was part of the new Yule tradition, a guide and mentor to the children of Iceland.

The transformation hadn't been just Grýla's—it had been theirs too.

"It feels strange," Þvörusleikir said softly, his long spoon clutched in his hands. "Not causing mischief anymore."

Askasleikir grinned. "Yeah, but I think I like this better. Helping the children learn, watching them grow—it's better than scaring them."

Kertasníkir, the Candle Stealer, held up a small candle, its flame flickering gently in the cold night air. "We've given them something more important than fear," he said. "We've given them hope."

Stekkjastaur looked around at his brothers, his heart swelling with pride. Each of them had found a new purpose, a new way to be part of Yule. They had learned that it wasn't enough to make children fear the season—they had to help them understand the true meaning of Yule: kindness, forgiveness, and the power of second chances.

"Do you think the children will remember us?" Stúfur asked, his voice small.

Giljagaur chuckled softly. "I think they will. But not in the way they used to. They won't remember us for the tricks we played or the fear we caused. They'll remember us for the lessons we taught."

Stekkjastaur nodded. "That's the legacy we're leaving behind. We've shown them that Yule isn't about being afraid. It's about learning, growing, and becoming better. That's something they'll carry with them long after this Yule is over."

The Yule Lads stood in quiet contemplation, the cold air swirling gently around them. The village was calm, the soft glow of candles in every window a reminder of the warmth and hope that had spread through the community.

Grýla's cave, once a place of fear, had become a gathering spot for families, where children listened to stories and learned the lessons of Yule from the once-feared ogress. The transformation was complete, and with it, the Yule Lads' roles had changed forever.

"I never thought we'd be here," Giljagaur said quietly. "But now that we are, I can't imagine going back to the old ways."

Stekkjastaur smiled. "Neither can I."

As the Yule Lads turned to leave the village, their hearts full of pride and hope, they heard a familiar voice behind them.

"Leaving already?"

They turned to see Grýla standing at the edge of the village, her cloak pulled tightly around her to keep out the cold. Her face, once hardened by years of anger and fear, was now softened by the warmth of the new Yule tradition. She had changed too, and the Yule Lads knew it.

Stekkjastaur smiled as he walked over to her. "We've finished our work, Mother," he said. "The children have learned their lessons."

Grýla nodded, her eyes filled with a quiet pride. "You've done well," she said. "All of you. I couldn't have asked for better sons."

The Yule Lads exchanged glances, their hearts swelling with warmth at their mother's words. For centuries, they had worked alone, playing tricks and causing mischief, but now, they were part of something much bigger— something that would last long after they were gone.

"We couldn't have done it without you," Stekkjastaur said softly. "You've shown us that even the most feared person can change."

Grýla smiled, a rare, genuine smile that reached her eyes. "And you've shown me that even the hardest hearts can soften."

The Yule Lads gathered around their mother, standing together as a family. The transformation wasn't just Grýla's—it was theirs too. They had all changed, and now they were leaving behind a legacy that would shape Yule for generations to come.

The next morning, as the first light of dawn broke over the snow-covered mountains, the Yule Lads prepared to leave the village and return to the wilderness where they lived. But this time, they weren't leaving behind fear or mischief. They were leaving behind something much more important.

As they walked away from the village, the soft glow of candles in the windows followed them, a reminder of the new Yule tradition they had helped create. The children would no longer fear Yule. Instead, they would look forward to it, knowing that it was a time of hope, of second chances, and of growth.

The Yule Lads had left their mark, and it was a legacy that would last long after the snow had melted and the winter had passed.

Stekkjastaur glanced back at the village one last time, his heart full. "We've done something good here," he said quietly.

Giljagaur smiled. "We have. And it's just the beginning."

Together, the Yule Lads walked into the mountains, the glow of Yule following them, a reminder of the hope and warmth they had brought to the village.

And as the sun rose higher in the sky, they knew one thing for certain: the legacy of the Yule Lads would live on, not as tricksters, but as bringers of light, hope, and second chances.

# Conclusion for Parents

As you've journeyed through this story of Grýla and the Yule Lads, there are a few important lessons to share with your children. At its heart, this tale is about second chances, kindness, and the possibility of change—even for the most unlikely characters.

You can remind your child that just like the children in the story, everyone has moments where they may misbehave or make mistakes. But, what really matters is learning from those mistakes and striving to become kinder, more compassionate people. The Yule Lads, known for their tricks and mischief, discovered that joy doesn't come from causing trouble, but from helping others and spreading kindness.

Here are a few discussion points you can explore with your child:

1. The Power of Kindness: Talk about how simple acts of kindness—like Bjarni helping the lost lamb or Inga sharing her milk—can make a big difference. Ask your child if they've ever experienced a moment where they showed kindness or if someone was kind to them, and how that felt.

2. Second Chances: Even characters like Grýla and the Yule Lads, who had a reputation for being mean or mischievous, were given a chance to change. This shows that everyone deserves an opportunity to learn from their mistakes and try again. Ask your child if there's ever been a time when they got a second chance to make things right, and what they learned from that experience.

3. The Spirit of Yule: The story emphasizes that Yule isn't just about gifts and fun—it's about reflecting on how we treat others. Encourage your child to think about how they can make their own Yule or Christmas season special by showing compassion and generosity, just like the children who got off Grýla's Naughty List.

By discussing these themes, you can help your child understand that the story is more than just a fun adventure. It's a reminder that, no matter what, we can always choose to be kinder, and that true change begins with small, thoughtful actions.

# Pronunciation Guide: Yule Lads

Stekkjastaur ("stye-kya-stoar")
The Sheep-Cote Clod, who harasses sheep with his stiff legs.

Giljagaur ("gil-ya-goar")
The Gully Gawk, known for sneaking into cowsheds to drink milk.

Stúfur ("stoo-fur")
The Small One or Stubby, who steals pans to lick the leftovers.

Þvörusleikir ("thvor-uhs-lay-kir")
The Spoon Licker, famous for sneaking into kitchens to lick wooden spoons.

Pottasleikir ("poat-ahs-lay-kir")
The Pot Scraper, who sneaks in to scrape the leftovers from pots.

Askasleikir ("ah-skahs-lay-kir")
The Bowl Licker, hiding under beds and waiting for bowls to lick clean.

Hurðaskellir ("hur-thah-skell-eer")
The Door Slammer, known for slamming doors during the night.

Skyrgámur ("skeer-gow-mur")
The Skyr Gobbler, who loves stealing skyr, a traditional Icelandic dairy product.

Bjúgnakrækir ("byoo-nah-kray-kir")
The Sausage Snatcher, always trying to steal sausages.

Gluggagægir ("gloo-ga-gye-geer")
The Window Peeper, who peeks into windows looking for things to steal.

Gáttaþefur ("gowt-tah-thev-ur")
The Doorway Sniffer, with a big nose and a love for the scent of baked goods.

Ketkrókur ("khet-krow-kur")
The Meat Hook, who uses a hook to steal smoked meat.

Kertasníkir ("ker-tah-sneek-eer")
The Candle Stealer, known for following children to steal their candles.

# Pronunciation Guide: Other Icelandic Names

Bjarni ("byar-nee")
A boy who learns compassion for the sheep he cares for.

Freyja ("frey-uh")
Snorri's younger sister, enjoying shared moments with him.

Grýla ("gree-lah")
The ogress of Yule, who punishes misbehaving children.

Inga ("eeng-ah")
A girl who learns generosity and sharing with her siblings.

Kári ("kow-ree")
A boy who learns the importance of helping out at home.

Leppalúði ("lep-pa-loo-thee")
Grýla's husband, a lazy giant who lives in the mountains with her.

Lóa ("loh-ah")
A girl who learns the value of sharing.

Marta ("mar-tah")
Inga's sibling, learning about sharing and kindness.

Sigrún ("sig-roon")
Lóa's younger sister who benefits from her sister's newfound generosity.

Snorri ("snor-ree")
A boy who learns fairness.

# History of the Icelandic Yule Lads

The Icelandic Yule Lads are a group of mischievous yet fun-loving characters from Icelandic Christmas traditions. These lads, originally known for their playful tricks, have changed over the years from being more scary to the friendly figures we know today. There are 13 Yule Lads, and they each visit children one by one in the 13 days leading up to Christmas.

Long ago, the Yule Lads were thought to be a bit naughty, causing trouble like stealing food or slamming doors. They lived in the mountains with their mother, Grýla, a giantess known for her scary nature, and their father, Leppalúði. Grýla was said to come down from the mountains to catch misbehaving children, but don't worry—this is just an old story! Today, the Yule Lads are much more playful and fun.

Each Yule Lad has his own special personality. For example, there's Stubby, who is very short and loves to steal pans to eat leftover crusts. Spoon-Licker enjoys sneaking into homes to lick wooden spoons, and Door-Slammer is known for slamming doors, especially at night, just for fun! They each take turns visiting homes, leaving small gifts for well-behaved children in their shoes, which are left on window sills.

Over time, the Yule Lads have become symbols of joy and holiday spirit in Iceland. They bring laughter, fun, and the excitement of Christmas. Children now look forward to their visits, knowing that a little treat might be waiting for them if they've been good.

Today, the Yule Lads are an important part of Icelandic Christmas traditions, reminding us that even though they once had a mischievous side, their playful nature brings cheer and happiness to the holiday season.

Made in the USA
Las Vegas, NV
04 December 2024

13355801R00063